5/5/08
to Peter —
thanks for being here,
and, as some american
said, "Let there be
commerce between
us"!
Cheers

GW00507516

SWEET POTATOES

{ selected stories }

LOU ROWAN

*aha***dada**

books

SWEET POTATOES

Copyright 2007 © Lou Rowan

All rights reserved. The use of any part of this publication transmitted in any form or by any means, electronic, mechanical, photocopying, recording, or otherwise, or stored in a retrieval system, without the prior consent of the publisher, is an infringement of the copyright law.

Jesse Glass, General Editor
Joe Zanghi, Production

First Edition
Printed and Bound in Canada

editorial addresses:

3158 Bentworth Drive
Burlington, Ontario
Canada L7M-1M2

Meikai University
8 Akemi, Urayasu-shi
Chiba-ken, Japan 279-8550

ISBN 978-0-9781414-5-5

For my mother, my sisters, my brother
and my stepmother.

Art Direction: Andrea Augé
Cover Design: Kevin Potis
Cover Photo: Brian Smale
Layout: Chris Hughes
Book Series Design: Daniel Sendecki

Thanks to the editors of Big Bridge, English Studies Forum, Friendly Local Press, Golden Handcuffs Review, the New Review of Literature, and Temenos, in which many of these stories first appeared.

CONTENTS

Introduction
to the Alphabet

I don't know whether I am more or less obsessed with me than the next guy with him. That's how I begin, at home usually with some words that move me—to the next words, some of which took me back towards my early days in California. Not once did I plan, although the truth is I am a planner, a plotter—an early-acquired and often useful mental habit in children of divorce. The bemused puzzlement I experience chasing the unexpected in these stories may be childish, adolescent, adult. Is the quest for mental and spiritual health a race with death?

But I want to say plainly that these stories *play* with autobiography, they entertain it. The game is a form, or better a quest for a formal flexibility, *not* a congeries of facts. I love everyone in my family, and want to thank them for all the fun I've had distorting their and my lives. I enjoy it when I'm asked after readings whether or not I was born with long red hair that scared my mother: the game continues. Huizinga's *Homo Ludens* and Bergson's *Laughter* explained much to me when I began to write. My life is not necessarily your business, but what I can make of it here might be. I sure hope so. And I love plot, character, surprise, *love* them.

GH

In hospitals the relationship between the machines, the instruments, the labyrinth of corridors, the rushing gowned bodies, the smells suggesting chemicals and secretions, and the human perceptual apparatus is exploratory at best. The unreason of hospitals is constant through history. To be a patient tests free will as radically as a family of origin.

G repeatedly passed out in medical circumstances. When he was young and drinking he saw a black-and-white movie, "The Brink of Life," and he couldn't withstand the threat of the birthing ward: he could smell the hospital in the Greenwich Village theatre, and left hastily to pass out by the curb on Bleeker Street. He passed out twice more in Village hospitals, once during day surgery to remove a ganglion bulging from his back, and once while his vas deferens was cut loose. He passed out as a teenager near Wilshire Boulevard when his oral surgeon showed him the incision, red like his imagination of a vagina, from which his wisdom teeth were being taken.

When he was admitted to the same Greenwich Village

hospital for an intestinal illness he was in pain and feverish. Access to his infection was through his sphincter, and preliminary information about its extent and nature was obtained manually. He sat for 2 hours in an examination room, to be joined not by his specialist but by 7 interns and residents, for St. Vincent's is a teaching hospital. Face down on a gurney, he was probed by each of the 7 as they discussed his infection, leaving their fingers in there as they talked. His anger and his pain prevented his fainting, but because he was unsure what lay ahead in this hospital he did not remove his anus from their fingers, even when they asked him questions implying that passage was a location of his sex life.

His specialist elected conservative treatment, which sounded reassuring to G. G visualized his intestine as a soft hose with a hole in it, surgery would tape or re-attach the ends of the hose, after which he would have a new set of pains to deal with, and a new set of explanations to present his visitors. His roommate in the semi-private suite was Hiram, an old man undergoing consistent attention from nurses and residents, requiring Hiram's bed to be curtained from G's. A nurse chuckled over Hiram, who was cantankerous and old, but her chuckle implied he had a right to be. Hiram was an improvement over Dave, who'd moved on to the cancer floor. Dave discussed endlessly his longing for Ray's Original Pizza, right around the corner, but forbidden to him. When Dave's wife visited, she said, "Now Dave, you know you can't have it." To which he would reply, "But it's *Ray's Original Pizza.*"

G felt bad about himself; he had a non-fatal and somewhat vague illness. G didn't know how to respond to Dave's cancer, but he noticed that Dave was apologetic too, apologetic to the doctors and nurses because he did not understand what they were about to do to him. Dave never asked why, he tried, haltingly, to grasp what.

Dave disappeared while G was exercising in the hall: 50 L-shaped laps pushing his IV post.

Hiram stared at G when his curtain was open, but did not respond when G greeted him politely. His skin was grey where his beard sprouted and pale ivory elsewhere, his legs and arms smooth like prosthetic devices.

G's continual objective was to make adjustments to his life that would make him feel good about himself: if he felt good physically, and even looked good, he would feel good generally. This hospital stay was progress towards the objective because he was not eating; conservative treatment dictated he give his bowels a rest, and his visitors marveled at his figure but derided his experimental mustache.

Talking with patients along the hall, G concluded that they saw themselves, sheepishly, as defective products, and his heart might have gone out to them did they not disappear, and did not he struggle not to believe everything inside him that wanted to agree with the hospital's treatment of him and them.

He longed for visits from his specialist, and for signs that his intestines were being treated. His worst moments were trivial: when he could not hold in the enema as long as the nurse demanded and rained from his bowels too soon; when he was kept waiting in an empty hall beyond the sonogram center for 2 hours, sitting on his sore spot in a wheelchair the orderly did not bother to brake, letting it glide towards the fire door until its rail bumped the dirty yellow wall and G, who had forgotten his book, facing the wall.

He longed to be walking, competent, jaunty like the doctor who showed him his sonogram, the bulge pressing his bladder. "*Mr. G, you're not pregnant are you!*" she exclaimed and he forced himself to laugh, but could find no riposte.

G's relief from his bodily and his general malaise was television and sleep. He began to find visits from friends oppressive, for they brought him back from stupor. He awoke at 2:00 AM to Hiram's voice. "Oh, Mama, MAMA." He awoke at 4:00AM, partially conscious of sounds of curtains, gurneys, bodies moving near him.

The nurse who couldn't exonerate G for his failed enema told G, "Oh him, he died."

For the rest of his stay G had the suite to himself. The pain in his intestine remained, but his temperature lowered, the internal symptoms, according to his specialist, ameliorated. Surgery would not be required. G felt forgiven by the hospital, but as he thought about his exoneration he realized that the hospital wouldn't have done it, it had to be something else.

I

I's bedroom was down the hall from his mother's; he slept
with his younger sister, who was behind a screen, a demarcation I
honored carefully. I remembers the screen, remembers the blackboard
easel on which he taught himself to write. His teachers were women;
he longed to please them. He shaped letters with slavish perfection at
the blackboard, was thrilled to have a few square feet of the classroom
in his bedroom. The capital "I" was, Mrs. T said, like a spoon at
the bottom, You began, careful always to work one continuous
stroke, by making a reverse small "l" but you DIDN'T STOP you
CONTINUED, "THAT'S RIGHT I DON'T STOP right through
the bottom of the spoon up about a quarter or third of the "l" and the
PAUSE at the tip of the crescent like the moon on its side, children,
and now STRAIGHT BACK ACROSS the board to the bottom of
the l-loop, and *look* how well I is doing it, I want you all to do it just
like I."

    I's sexual fantasies were purposeful. He brought girls from
his classroom to join girls from the neighborhood, mostly friends of

his sister, into his enlarged bed, and he taught them. Authoritative, he taught them how to pee properly, which generally required he demonstrate the strength of his stream. His heart went out to the girls, the impulse to teach them humming through him. He taught them to overcome the mistakes that came so naturally to girls, putting their clothes on when they should be off, for example, or paying attention to each others' silliness when their whole beings should be fastened on an I transfixed by his calling to teach them.

I remembers his mother singing in the kitchen, her voice so lovely he thought she was the radio, and she chuckled when he told her that. He was struggling in the patio with his assignment from his stepfather to tie a bowline knot. He succeeded after weeks of tearful frustration when he found an illustrated knot-book, and the little arrows in the diagram taught him the way that in his stepfather's fast-moving or even slow-moving hands eluded him.

He forgave ugly girls in his fantasies. A girl on his schoolbus named Becky worked at the cannery. He brought her to bed and held her scaly hands, forcing her to give them up to him, filling her with strength to acknowledge them. Masterful, he disciplined his disgust for her fishy smell, her rough flesh, her harsh name.

I remembers the hallway separating his bedroom from the living room and the kitchen. He knows it led to his mother's bedroom, but he cannot remember her end of the hall, or the bedroom. He remembers noxious smells from his mother's bathroom, but not the bathroom.

I remembers dinner: the table set neatly, the butter-dish and the huge beaded glass of whole milk flanking the silverware, the chafing-dishes of vegetables, potatoes, pastas, boats of sauces, gravies all waiting, like I and his sister, for the adults to arrive, and then seat themselves properly, lifting the chairs carefully across the thick shag rug, so as not to jerk them, as I had, into the table and spill the tall glasses.

If there was soup, the extra spoon to be dipped away from I's body but delicately tipped towards his lips, a little insuck of air to pull it in, but it is not to be blown on. The salad-fork was smaller than the main-course fork, and salad was easier to take in, required fewer corrections or directions from I's mother than soup, but it was boring compared to what he wanted: the meats she served, especially hamburger tastefully enhanced with fragments of bread and onion, ham sweetly glazed, roast beef in plate-size slices. The tiny salt-spoon dropped the salt in clumps I tried furtively to spread across the juicy surface. Artichokes were fun because of the melted butter and because you could use your fingers, more fun than bread because the butter must be spread so thin you couldn't taste it, or because the butter-pat was unsalted.

I tended to lose concentration, and would be caught picking at his vegetables, sawing them with his fork-tines, rather than taking the trouble to pick up his properly-angled knife, or racing through the meat, only to become "full" in the middle of the vegetables.

B was his sister's friend, her father a doctor. B was a hero at this table because she was of such exemplary politeness: she finished everything served her (though she was small and thin unlike I and his sister), politely accepting seconds, but even more because on two occasions she excused herself to hasten to the bathroom through the kitchen to throw up. When I had boils, B's father lanced them, and instructed him on bringing their pus to the surface with hot compresses. I can still find the scars on his legs, shoulders, and wrist from the boils.

Seconds were a painful decision for I: balancing his shifting perceptions of what his mother wanted against what was happening inside his shirt and trousers.

Dessert was sweet but often too complex, too adult. I's ideal sweets were brownies, which his mother made so rich you could stand the walnuts, Hershey bars without nuts, or frozen Snickers bars. Eskimo pies were good until I ate near the wood stick.

Stewed fruit was a frustrating dessert, warm but not sweet enough. Apple and cherry pie were tart, but a la mode they were perfect: huge, and satisfying to stupefaction.

Dessert took less time than the early courses, and while working at it I knew that, once he had carefully cleaned his plate, done everything he possibly could within his skill-set to clear the table and tidy up , he could sink into relative relaxation on the sofa before the TV, and during commercials he would allowed into the icebox for more dessert, should he rinse his dish properly, and he knew that his mother's attention would be directed towards the screen, not towards him and his sister. And maybe it would be Red Skelton or Lucy, and he could giggle unchecked.

L

for Spencer Holst

L intended to marry his college sweetheart and that didn't work, but after he dropped her she produced their son, who failed to interest him. He became president of his family's company, which went south, his career with it, and his relatives, alleging improprieties, pursued him like balance sheet furies. He tried writing, but failed to keep his children's-books free of his bitterness. He studied the history, ecology, and the political economy of his region as, dependent on the girlfriend who materialized while he was president, he became more and more expert on how the world works.

He damned his lineage and his luck. When he reached 50 he went on a diet and worked out rigorously in Gold's gym. His hair receded but his musculature was that of a college boy. His girlfriend was promoted, and they moved to a suburban house from which she could commute downtown to her actuarial duties. His files of crucial information filled the house, and it became embarrassing to entertain—not a problem because her work busied her so, and because his bitterness increased with his knowledge. He felt himself constantly on the edge of the discovery his mental and physical exercise brought ever nearer.

His relatives believed he was addicted to cocaine. The closer we get by blood or involvement, the less we know L, a principle governing the acuity of L-awareness from relatives to siblings to his mother, who disowned him, and to L himself.

I am his brother; I am struggling with my poverty of emotional insight. But I am a protestant brought up to believe that effort is its own reward, and I have persisted to the brink of putting my brother's case to bed.

In June of 2004 our collective western culture absorbed a shock worse than a body blow. Bob Dylan, whose purity of intentions is a pillar or at least a brick in our cultural edifice, sold out, lending his wrinkled grizzled image to advertisements for underwear covering while uncovering the breasts and pelvises of women young enough to be his grandchildren. My brother believes deeply in Bob Dylan.

Secondly, my wife was a textile designer before computers outsourced her work to themselves, and she designed the tissue paper that nestles against the underwear to which Bob Dylan scandalously lent his haggard visage.

My wife has two pairs of panties from this company, one purple, one emerald. Each sports a small bow in line with her navel. The flesh around her navel is softer and smoother than my dreams of flesh. The panties have remained fresh and shapely since 1993, unlike any other panties in our collection of underwear—I'm certain because I wash them.

My brother works at home, like me. His girlfriend's name, like that of many of her upper-bourgeois protestant coevals, could be a man's name, and it is associated with the finer grades of a precious metal. Bob Dylan is a pseudonym. If you look at the covers of his early legendary acoustic albums, you see the pleasantly hermaphroditic image of Puer, or of a clown.

My wife's name is very feminine, as is its diminutive, and it can be associated with British royalty, with intercessory religious icons, and with a wealthy American colony.

When Woody Guthrie, Bob Dylan's icon, wrote about the famous river he so fluently and movingly sent to "roll on" through our hearts, he was in the pay of Uncle Sam, whose engineers were blasting and scraping to dam that river, inundating lands and caves sacred to the humans closest to native on this continent.

I cannot say that I have made a surplus of overtures to my estranged brother, but I have made all the overtures, and when we are together it is painful, for as he makes his points about political economy, about his luck and his lineage, he hits me on my biceps and triceps with the backs of his fingers.

It is clear to me as I ponder these clues that my brother's crisis, or stasis, stretching back to before the record bull markets we have enjoyed, has to do with his substituting Bob Dylan for his father, confusing Bob Dylan with his brother, putting Bob Dylan between him and his son, between him and his lover.

When I graduated from college, I went to a liberal protestant seminary in New York; I always intended to do good. My use of cocaine back East was minimal and unsatisfactory.

I do my best to forgive my brother for his malevolence

towards me, and towards my sisters, mothers, fathers, uncles and cousins. I thank God for inventing secular humanism during the renaissance and the reformation, for it has freed me to worship the fertile field of my wife's belly--and not the false prophecies of a commercial icon the condemnation of whose repulsive image is inevitable to anyone who beholds it adjacent to the exposed flesh of once-innocent maidens sacrificed to the Moloch of our popular culture.

M

Ms. M loved her first name, despite its traditional protestant origin.

She loved its irreducibility, as she called it: her freedom from nicknames and diminutives based on it. Yes, she had been called reserved, supercilious, formal--and thus Miss Priss, Our Miss Manners, or just Manners--and by her enemies, Man.

When she and her partner "became pregnant" they kept it to themselves how that was effected. Her friends and acquaintances clucked, "Just like Our Miss Priss," assigning her yet again to another century and debasing her social currency.

But M and her partner managed a foundation in the billions. They served on the boards of important endowments, and between them there was no cause in their state sanctioned by anything save sects wishing to rule the country's crotches to which they did not contribute their expertise, their resources, and their presence.

Never did M or her partner ever aver or ever assume in any nuance of any assertion or repartee that their union, technically illegal in their state, effused any oddness.

They were hikers, and they walked or bicycled to work in all weathers. Their being with child did not manifest itself until the third month, when a slight alteration in M's tastefully-plain clothing revealed that she was the "we" who carried their firstborn.

M and her partner inflicted social awkwardness: in their presence, gossip—the emollient, the lubricant the luxuriant fruits of society squeeze from and apply to themselves—was denied the visages of conversation They allowed themselves to ask, "How are you," but if your suffering was not an infection or virus, a cellular rampage, a muscular or skeletal infraction, the death of a loved one, they would steer the conversation with polite subtlety to topics not limited to you—or them. They uttered the term "society" regularly, but by it they denoted the entire polis, and they breathed adamantine certainty that society's consciousness and sensitivities were defined by the causes to which they contributed.

Further abrasive was their laughter. M's partner's ranged from a mule-like bellow to a chime-like giggle, and M ranged from a percussive cackle to a whinny fast as automatic gunfire. They covered their mouths and they excused themselves, but they could not prevent their joy from feeling, to the majority of what the press called society, a judgment.

Because M and her partner were present, conspicuously, at all significant social gatherings, you could discuss them only at small discrete affairs. A graduate of the finest ladies' college here, now as a society reporter for the state's finest liberal journal, estimated that M and partner were topics at 85% of private parties that mattered. And she confided to me what discomposed her circle the most profoundly,

"They're touchers! How can they be such touchers? Good *god* their hands are all over each other. Nothing naughty, but *still.* . . . And they're just as bad with me, and everybody! They squeeze your arm, lean on your shoulder, slam you on the back—lord when she was orating on, oh please, 'social conscience' M put her hand right on an old lady's sternum as she thanked her for her so-called 'great heart.' Jesus, there must have been 20 of us who expected her to honk the old buzzard's wrinkled breast."

The relationship between personality and genetics is mind-numbingly-complex. It is known that addictions run in families, but there is little research on inheritance and sexual proclivity, or on genetics and social eccentricity.

But I have discovered M's secret. She is a lineal descendent of Lambert Strether. She suffers from none of Strether's historian's unwillingness to name the source of his fortune: the finest toilet valves ever invented, valves whose airtight patent holds to this day, protected by a growling pack of intellectual property lawyers M and her partner periodically sic upon boutique producers of the highest-end commodes.

M's partner descends from Henry Ward Beecher, on the sinister side.

Given the origins of their and most other fortunes and fames, it has rarely occurred to M, whose given name is Charity, to take herself seriously --although she can understand and tolerate it when we do.

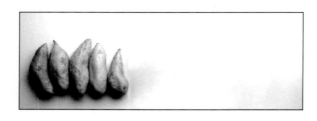

O

Ordinarily is a bold word, denoting and connoting most of life. If we can find in our experience an order speaking to all men, we are blessed.

I am an alcoholic, which makes me a systematic thinker. The chaos of my inner being, whatever he is, requires I impose a strictures upon myself.

I banged my head against the living-room wall yesterday at 4:07 PM, denting the sheetrock. My girlfriend walked out, past my bleeding brow, my bloody shirt, and I was free of her to drink until I woke in my blood, urine, and vomit on the couch nearest the dent. An artist down from Vermont was ringing the doorbell. I forgot he was coming. He'd built his own house in the wilderness; he grew his own vegetables; he was thin, wiry, and would sleep with my girlfriend. He was amused by the empty jug at my feet. He showed me the work he'd sold to a publisher of famous cookbooks and to *the New Yorker.*

My girlfriend had a vision of sweat equity. You bought an

old house, you restored it, and you and the house were better for it. In my orderly universe this made sense, like the bicycle I bought to save fuel and exercise my quads and my heart. The helmet was hot in the summer heat, and Brooklyn was hillier than I noticed walking or driving. The renovation was an intricate series of boring tasks, and so I hoped to get my girlfriend pregnant so she would stop working with the noxious wood-stripping chemicals, but drunk I was repugnant and sober I was impotent.

I banged my head against the sheetrock with which I had reluctantly replaced the spongy plaster because my girlfriend had been right. In an orderly universe, when you have no answer you begin a new conversation.

She was right that I was doing little work on the house, was getting drunk whenever convenient, was unreliable at parties, falling asleep and peeing on couches, leaving her to take the late subway home.

We retain an inner child that manifests itself when we need it. This summer I was exploring, with the help of a therapist who looked like a rock star, the evolution of my inner order, and it was early in our work. I had agreed that my girlfriend should control the checkbook. She wrote the checks to the therapist.

Inner children are instruments of a sensitivity multiples of the sensitivity of grown-ups. When my girlfriend's anger exploded into rage, I was like a seismograph beside an erupting crater. I had hoped she could understand it would take time for the outrages visited upon my sensitivities by my 4 parents to be assuaged by the therapeutic rock star.

The artist was patient in his work and competent with his

hands. He was shorter than I, and sinewy. I was portly from the beer and wine. I told the therapist that I thought of the artist's body as an erection, and his competence as a stone wall. The therapist said, "Wow, let's go with that. Tell me about your associations with erections and stone walls."

Once upon a time I lived in a little house on a small lot in the sand in a small beach town near the Pacific Ocean. In this town there were many vacant lots between the small houses where we boys would play touch or tackle football, and where we would build forts from which we would bomb each other with sticks and rocks and bags of sand that acted like fallout. One day an older boy and I stood behind the forts and threw rocks at each other from what seemed a safe distance. Always in my youth I enjoyed throwing things, and I could skip rocks farther than any of my buddies. I hit the older boy square between the eyes at his hairline, the rock bounced about ten feet in the air, and I was running home barefoot and he was chasing me with a rock in each fist. My house had a wood gate framed by cinderblocks painted green. As the older boy called me names I taunted him from behind the gate, and he launched a rock at me that banged the wood loudly and I scurried inside worried my mother would blame that scar in the hardwood gate on me.

Now I worried my sense of order rendered me incapable of responding to therapy.

When my girlfriend returned that night, the artist kissed her warmly on each cheek but I can't remember the evening because his being there meant I was free to drink, and free to go to bed by myself without her confronting me about anything. In bed I imagined finding a new girlfriend, before sleeping 12 hours.

The next day was sunny and hot, and my girlfriend and the artist were enjoying coffee. Perspiring, I sipped coffee, imagining it would eliminate the mild vestiges of the hangover the long sleep had attenuated. I did not care that I could not follow their discussion of the current art scene, for I knew that the plastic arts were dominated by money not talent, an absurdity that closed the scene to my logic. I excused myself to return to my research on inner-city language-patterns, a sure-fire source of funding from my liberal school. I was drunk when I made the proposal to the school board, but they thought I was profound. I converted to the school's religion, sensing job security in devotion.

Order dictates logic, which dictated my plans.

The books on inner-city language took its patterns back to Africa. I had studied linguistics for my masters, but I couldn't remember the phonetic alphabet, so that the music and meaning of the sonic evolution eluded me, just as serenity had on my bike.

The artist and my girlfriend went to Manhattan to do the galleries. His younger son had been run over out of his wife's hand, then taken to a hospital in Harlem that neglected him as he lay in the crowded hall with ruptured organs. His death drove them from New York to the Vermont hillside, where she joined a crowd of adult children dealing to the liberal women's college, and began sleeping with an exceptionally hairy and irresponsible man, leaving the artist with the older son, who began designing comics starring Nazis and aerial bombardment. The speech-patterns of the peripheral adult children imitated, inconsistently, those of the inner city. The artist's wife was very beautiful, and I knew no one, including me, who did not want to sleep with her. I was always faithful to my girlfriend because I was unsure I could perform upon anyone else.

But the old house had water-pipes running outside the structural walls through an unheated outbuilding, and in severe cold they could freeze and burst. It was my task to insulate the outbuilding, or the pipes, but I couldn't do it, and I sat with books about inner-city language in my lap, a bottle at my feet, imagining floods running into the remote crawl space full of dust and rat feces. The artist or my handy renovating neighbors could deal with the pipes, taking responsibility for their integrity like good brownstone pioneers. But I could not face the complexity of the task, the contempt of the bluff locals in the hardware store. And so in orderly fashion I took my biggest raincoat from the downstairs closet and covered my lap with it. Then I cut my right wrist with a double-edge razor blade, cutting also the fingers with which I sawed at myself, incompetent to the last. The goodly flow made me dizzy, and I folded the coat over my right arm and waited to die.

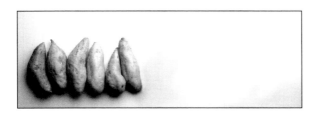

P

Men have it easier than women. Barring a stiff wind, they pull it out and let go. Their role in reproduction is limited to putting it in, and then, in 73% of the cases, observing the crescent results with appreciation and pride. They faint in delivery rooms while their mates push and scream.

P would like to do something about these disparities, which the prevalence of prostate cancer only underscores, for its onset is later and its treatment less disfiguring than the equivalent in women's breasts. He wakes up guilty most mornings, amazed at his wife's capacity for pain and inconvenience. He has never hesitated to buy her sanitary napkins.

His wife rarely complains. Her comments on what the media call "women's issues" are even scarcer, focusing on affronts to women's dignity, not their bodies' humiliations. P is grateful to his wife for her mature stoicism, but he proceeds, as I say, with a guilty, tentative quality in his morning overtures to her, a hesitation she adores, for it separates him from the brash obtuseness of his gender. But her loving his hesitancy, which he will not compliment himself by calling humility, fails to eradicate P's inhibitions as he exercises his freedom to micturate and essays consequence-free lovemaking.

But again he is blessed, for his wife loves his inhibitions, the shy awkwardness of his approach to her body.

And so P, whose capacity for original expression is narrow, paused last Sunday at noon, his wife breathing softly and deeply next to him in their moist bed—paused I say after touching his fingertips to his loins and savoring her smell on them, and with joy an idea but not a feeling thought, *Really, P, what's wrong with this picture?* And he recognized, for in this moderately exalted state novel visions entered P, that it was not his fault that his wife's labia, his genitals and (he would soon see in the mirror) his lips were flecked with blood. He recognized with the force of insight that he did not cause the walls of his wife's womb to break down and issue from her as blood.

P's sense of humor, habitually self-directed, empowered him to smile at his confusing himself with God or with the program that dictates evolution. *That's a good one, P,* he thought.

And this Sunday it occurred to him how many of his male friends were gay. He regretted that Hollywood had not as yet given him a clearer picture of how gay men make love; he could not imagine embracing and licking rough hairy skin. He mused on most gay couples saving themselves the pains of reproduction, but then he remembered HIV, and the twinge of guilt impelled him to roll ever so gingerly from the bed, leaving his wife, whose breathing in sleep was so quiet and smooth he wanted to cry, undisturbed.

In the bathroom he peed in the sink, to help the environment by using less water to flush, and to preserve the quiet that would preserve his wife's rest.

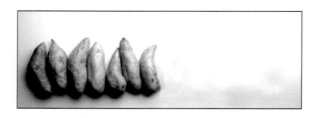

T

to Rover

Nowhere was it more apparent than his shirt-front: T was a sloppy eater. The most graceful leading man in the Seattle Ballet Company, the finest lyric poet of the Northwest, could not keep food off his face and his clothing. I have never in my 5 decades of work in the arts seen the mundane so threaten the sublime. I would rather be caught in an opium den or beneath the ministrations of a lap-dancer than appear an embarrassing slob at banquets. T has been my most trying, exasperating problem as the PR and fund-raising manager for the merged Seattle Ballet and Seattle Center for the Arts.

The rich demand visitations from the stars in return for their donations. In the arts fundraising rules the politics, and public relations governs stardom. It is customary for leading men and divas to grasp the bejeweled bodies or suffer the clutches of major donors on polished dance floors. It is customary for them to make pretty little inarticulate speeches of thanks in heavy Slavic accents, standing above the banquet for all to adore.

Contemplating T's white ruffles in these situations was a nightmare, for T was blessed with a metabolism whose velocity allowed him to eat copiously of whatever he wanted; his favorites were sauces, gravies, soups, red meats, red wines, anything "decadent and gorgeous."

Worst of all for me was the annual banquet at the lumber heiress's mansion. The lumber heiress funded anything worth funding in Seattle arts, fuelling not only her husband's fame as a developer but also his reputation as a donor to aesthetic causes whose marmoreal locations were adorned with his name. She sat sphinx-like in the background as he basked in his notoriety, and very few of us mendicants of the spirit were privileged to meet her. Her reserve, her dignity, the abrupt simplicities of her conversation allowed or forced her husband and increasingly her precocious son whose mini-projects she backed to speak for her. It was as if she was a female Jove: we all sought her cataclysmic nod.

And the pure palor of her skin, emerging at the chiseled upper portion of her bust from a gown so tastefully-wrought for the occasion as to be the subject of articles in the dailies and a spread in the good-living monthly, was an alabaster reminding one of classical statuary from which time and weather have removed the paint. The glorious gown was in a cream tone that was richness itself.

She left speechmaking at the annual Banquet of the Arts to her son and to select guests, her central position at the head table on a slightly elevated chair defining her peerless station, from which she made bland but trenchant conversation with her two guests of honor, of whom T was the most prominent on her right.

I ate at what my competitors and I called the table of prostitution, and as I exchanged the expected lies with them about the growth of my endowments tripling the growth of my fixed costs, I hoped they could not notice the fear my practiced mannerisms disguised, but which my occasionally-husky voice and my subsiding into monotones could betray.

I was so right to be afraid.

There was my most prominent client, my star, my fundraising magnet rising above the goddess of Seattle wearing a white tie and white shirt polluted by drippings from each of the five courses preceding the pre-Chateau d'Yquiem palate cleansers. There he was taking bows with fragments of Kobe beef dropping from his front. There he was forgetting his glass of red wine in his hand, and emptying it onto the heiress' right shoulder, from which it ran onto her gown like an opened artery. The collective intake of breath, the little shrieks of dismay, the rush of obsequious guests to minister were suddenly quelled by the hostess's slapping away the hands hovering nearest her and in a voice that slight graceful frame somehow managed to amplify into brazen, raucous tones of unadulterated anger: "TAKE YOURS HANDS OFF! Get AWAY from me! Take your seats! *Please resume, Maestro T.*"

The rest is a blurred nightmare. I remember the utter silence into which T deployed his gracefully-rueful apologies and continued his whimsical remarks about how our hostess had with singular magic converted Seattle's life of the spirit from a swampy fly-blown estuary to a humming electrified metropolis, concluding with mock-heroic couplets on her and her family. And I remember the smirks of my table-mates.

After what I kept saying to myself was the mercy-killing that finally released us from the party, I removed my jacket and tie, dropped my braces, and slumped into my corner of the wide back seat of the limo, refusing to speak as T poured me champagne from the ice bucket.

At home, I burst into tears.

"How can you do this do me? How can you ruin all my work with these revolting displays. Everything was ruined, ruined, because you insist, you the most graceful man on earth, you insist on soiling yourself like an infant in a high chair. This is tragic, tragic."

But he picked me up and carried me from the foyer to the bedroom.

"Hush, hush, my little boy. My little I, you know it's not a tragedy, you know the event was perfect, wonderful, and all those beautiful people are in love with everything you do, as am I."

And as he lowered me gently to our bed I remembered how much strength it takes to be a dancer.

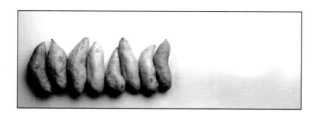

V

for James Tierney

The building is near Union Station. Good move guys, V thinks, you can get cheap labor here easy. The lobby is dominated by a series of black marble slabs, water dribbling over and bubbling up between them.

The receptionist is a Black woman poured into a skimpy halter and a cowgirl miniskirt, her face a mask of gray-purple makeup, her manner so stylized and self-involved he can't even begin to buddy up to her the way he has to so many girls who've given him tidbits on entering so many corridors of power. The coffee she implies he'd better drink is putrid, and he's about to ask for the Men's when the receptionist's seeming twin scoops him up and he struggles to match her long strides through a corridor in black and white stripes ending at glass inserted like a flat plug to the hall, giving a stunning view as he nears overcoming confusion the stripes running by him and the women instill, suddenly turning right down a corridor he hadn't noticed to the row of executive offices, each of which is plugged by the same giant pane giving on the hectic panorama of Seattle's origin.

He's wondering if he should have gone for the white collar and sharp cuffs with the black pinstripe, when she stops, and he strides past her towards a man he can't see clearly in the glare of his glass, but knows is Victor Vector himself, and V thinks he's got the job if he's already *in* with the company's driving force.

Vector ignores his outstretched hand, continues typing on his minicomputer, talking softly into a mike attached to his collar. His assistant steps behind his massive black slab-marble desk to untangle the wire from his left cufflink, which flashes in the brightness from the now-cloudless sky and the blue bay.

V strains to hear Vector, groping for tidbits, but the voice is like an indivisible white noise.

The seats are backless black benches, and V takes one uninvited, leaning in to take this guy on.

Vector's preoccupation lasts long enough that V strains to hold his aggressive poise, concentration muddled by his bladder. Vector removes the little mike and still typing murmurs, "Yes?"

"Sir, it's a privilege to meet you. I'm here to help you grow your vital business."

"Yes?"

Vector is fair-skinned, and if he were white would be called a nerd, the kind of ordinary man the technical industries have held up, as in the amorphous persons of Paul Allen and Bill Gates, to be the visual symbols of modern business. But because he is Black, his features grate, do not compose themselves into the routinely undistinguished Americanism on the covers of the business press.

When Vector speaks, something happens in his nasal cavity that sounds like an insucking of phlegm, and V can't resist his disgust with a Black nerd with rhinitis.

"I think we can grow this exciting enterprise right into the Fortune 500."

"How?"

"I think China and the Tigers and Europe are great markets for you. I'd avoid the expense of Japan."

"Why?"

"Mr. Vector, those markets are believers in the old US of A. They're huge investors in our debt."

"I know. What does that have to do with growing Vulgate?"

"Sir, you've got to go a. where you're wanted and b. where there's a scarcity of your product."

"Obviously. Proceed."

V knows Vector will not notice his flush and moisture because he's not raised his eyes from his little screen.

"Well, when I take over sales here, I'm going to use my culture and experience to find salesmen from each market to grow your lines."

"That didn't work in Africa."

"Excuse me, but I think Africa and Latin America are not ready for your products."

"Why not?"

"You need to go where there's an established or a newly-growing middle class."

"OK, go on."

Vector continues to type. There is no change in the pace of his fingers. V cannot tell if Vector is recording his ideas, ignoring him, what.

"In Asia I'd raid the computer service sector for talent ready to make the next step."

V is proud of himself for thinking of that one. Vector types on.

"In Europe I'd do what we do in America, raid the big banks—they're great breeders of talent they can't keep."

Wow, he's on a roll. He decides to stop and wait Vector out.

"OK, thanks, we might call you."

"Mr. Vector, I'm eager to work with you. Is there anything else you would like to know about me?"

"No thanks."

"May I plan on calling you next week, Sir."

"Fine. Fine." The "i's" elicit the sounds in Vector's nose.

V turned the wrong way in the hall, but righted himself after emerging into a vast bright amphitheater of sloppily-dressed ugly young people working on black benches at black pods randomly-placed on gray industrial carpet. Their voices were low, and V felt he was passing out of consciousness, but his nervous anger and the pain below sustained him until he found his way past the preoccupied semi-naked receptionist, into the impressive atrium, where he felt that his long experience in business was a sham, he was idiotic to think he could compete in today's market, his shirt chafed his neck, and he hoped his fucking family was grateful to him for exposing himself like this, he'd never do it if it weren't for them.

That night he dreamed was visiting his mother and stepfather, and he was happy to be home. He walked briskly to his stepfather, whom he hoped was proud of the business career he'd sustained after so many false starts in life. He embraced his stepfather, who submitted to his enfolding arms reluctantly, and at the last instant thwarting their closing with hands to his biceps, and turned from him to something behind V's left shoulder. V turned and saw the parents of a girl he'd dated long ago waving and pointing at V. His stepfather admitted them to the sunroom giving on the bay, where yachts like the one he and V had sailed to Catalina Island maneuvered in a tight race in the brisk breeze.

The parents were followed by the young woman, who was crying, her head drooping abjectly.

"What can we do? What can we do? Look at her cry. She's been weeping and waiting all this time for your son to marry her."

The homecoming was no longer the joy he'd permitted himself to hope for, a flood of celebration for his promotion at the big bank.

His stepfather asked for an explanation, his mother stationed at the door to the sunroom.

V forced a laugh, and used all his sales skills. "Surely no one believes the offhand remark of a teenager to be a commitment for life, surely you jest."

He thought that was a good one that would carry the day with his stepfather and restore joy to the homecoming because his stepfather was nothing if not sensible. But no his stepfather silently turned his head from V to the outraged father who was saying, "Why? Why do so many women find him attractive?"

V decided to take a walk, to let them all sort it out. None of the streets connected as he expected them too, and the renovations by his schoolboy friends to homes whose outsides and patios he had adopted and counted on during his walks when he still lived here and needed to get away expanded them to such vast styles they became part of the road-

system, which tunneled under them or elevated itself to ramps around them, affording V no place to walk, and so he went home and looked in the window at the girl, who being still as young as she was 25 years ago appeared very attractive, and he decided to solve his life's problems and please everyone in his home by marrying her, but his best friend met him by the door, his best friend who had always succeeded in business from the time he read V's stepfather's castoff Wall Street Journals *as a precocious preteen, and reminded V he was already married and had 5 children. "That's not a good idea, V."*

V never knew why he remembered some dreams and forgot others.

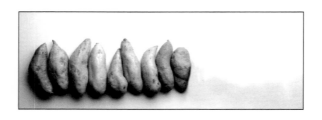

W

I pull my undergarments from their nestling-place, handling
with aplomb pieces of cloth that billions extract daily from their
nightly limpness, each one of us alone with hands, cloth, crotch,
buttocks, belly. When my life was in a deadly chaos, I weighed 25
pounds more than I do now, and the shiny vertical lines above my
pubic hair are witness. I look at my ass in the full-length mirror, and
I'm impressed by its rounded musculature, its smooth whiteness, but
disappointed by the fleshy folds where it joins my thighs. I turn my
back to the mirror, stretching to look for my scars, but the fatty folds
above my pelvis distract me, and I wish that my skin could descend
from my chest past my defined ribs to my hips in a smooth muscular
sweep, and I decide that the diet I am beginning today will make me
an exception to rules governing male flesh.

When I was young we tanned ourselves each summer, not as
Malcolm X has said, in tribute to the superiority of black skin, but
because that was our custom in California, and because we believed
a deep tan covered our zits. It bothers me when a woman's face has

been roughened by acne, and I am happy to have been born after the demise of smallpox. As I shave my somewhat-pocked face, I try to remember how I got the scar under my prominent chin, I look for signs of drooping flesh below my jaw, and I notice the mottling of my forearms, the age-spots joining the scars from my boils and the stab-wound from my sister's pencil.

The stretch marks are unresponsive, but if my fingers stray lower, the flesh does respond, and I wonder what other men think, what other men feel, when they wash their genitals, when they put them into underwear, when they adjust them to avoid pains caused by the pressure of trousers or thighs.

Dressing is a soliloquy.

I cannot imagine—well, I can because I did it in boarding-school and sleep-away camps--dressing without privacy, something I know billions do not have.

My sister stabbed me because I was taunting her. I was bigger than she, and threats boys from my little world would laugh at dismayed her. Just as my mother could make me cringe by scolding or make me cower by spanking me, I could drive my sister crazy by picking up her chocolate Easter egg and pretending to take a big bite from it, by chuckling over the top half of her bathing suit when she had no breasts, by pinning her arm behind her back in a hammerlock, by firing my cap-gun next to her ear, by threatening to burst into the bathroom when she was on the toilet, by telling her she would get fat and get pimples as she ate her second dessert, by calling her names like dope and dummy, by telling her I heard Mom tell our stepfather she'd been bad so she wasn't getting any Christmas presents, by telling her the bathroom smelled when she'd been in it, by shooting her with rubber-tipped arrows, by blocking the television, by dumping her favorite dolls from her dresser to the floor, by marking up pictures she colored, by telling her how ugly and weak girls are.

The wood pencil broke off on my radius, and I removed the lead tip from my forearm, howling more in outrage than pain. I hit her a roundhouse right to the stomach, and the babysitter attended to her not me as she lay on the carpet gasping, despite the hole in my skin.

X = Y + Z ?

In math we speak of *plotting* curves. Authorities on the unknown like scientists and physicians are first person plural, "We treat your symptoms with protocols A and B, and generally we achieve satisfactory results." We fit lines known as curves, even when they are straight, to the data. We are reassured by their stories, our imagined place in the plot's diagram.

We can simulate not only human and animal behavior but also the entire cosmos and its history on powerful computers. Yesterday a scientist called a computer's model of a supernova, "a brave calculation."

Fear of the unknown impels us to reason, reasons, reasoning. Hostages with weapons next their skins beg their captors to understand they had nothing to do with what outrages their captors. They quake, vomit, piss and crap, but they go on talking, hoping their words will plot their future.

When I was in college I suffered the math fear that is said to afflict women, and so I took a course on the history of science, rather than a lab course. I learned that the Ptolemaic system explains most everything visible in the visible heavens. But I was impatient with Professor Cohen, because I wanted to know the truth.

It takes, we are told, a wall to cause a white dwarf to explode. The semiotics of the sentence I just wrote is beyond me.

Few words that have meaning to me, like *feelings, serenity, peace, comfort, love,* and *meaning* can survive radical analysis.

I experience life as a radical analysis of me. It would be bathetic to compare myself to a hostage, but it would be inaccurate to say that comfort and meaning occur naturally or frequently to me. If you ask me, how are you, you have imposed a problem on me I cannot solve. And you will never stop asking me how are you.

My father would interrupt my boyhood complaints to declare, *There is no such thing as "can't."* Had I the time I would plot my life to test that hypothesis The X axis would be Failure and the Y axis not Success but Achievement or Completion. And if I could plot a representative sample of my life's discrete events and projects, increased steepness of the curve would represent validation of Dad's dictum. I would need scientific advice on how to define each term.

Then I might know whether my feelings are true or false.

And we would have a story I could never write, for I can't plan, but which we could all accept, as we watch my scientific and medical advisors project the data and demonstrate their plotting with the red eyes of their laser pointers.

And were they my readers, I would ask them to please excuse my good intentions, which I am unable to veneer. If they cannot, they'll close me and put me down. But they should know that I will feel it when they abandon me.

They can hold me and exclaim over me. They can kiss my outside—even my innards.

It is assumed that I should nourish them, but the neediness that propels my good intentions is voracious.

To be frank as good intentions dictate: my story tells of consistent deprivation. My parents forgot to baptize me, perhaps because my shock of long red hair drove my young mother to faint at the sight of her firstborn.

I look at my birth certificate from the Good Samaritan in Los Angeles, at the prints of my little feet, and I'm overwhelmed by love for all the babies I see in restaurants and parks, babies whose attention I solicit by imitating their little moves with their mouths their toys their little fingers. I know they cannot see me clearly, and they will not remember me.

From the first there were caretakers for me, English, Scotch, and German. One had been my mother's nanny. My mother is alive, the caretakers dead, like my father.

Privation differs from deprivation: I always ate well, too well.

But I was always at a loss.

I was at a loss to tune my feelings to what came at me from my parents, or what didn't. I received plenty of guidance on manners and table manners, which serves me in good stead to this day.

At a loss and awkward. Which led to self-consciousness, shyness, and to loneliness.

I'm not clear on what led to what.

And this is not so much a letter to the world as an intercourse with it, whose pages reek of the games, the songs, the comfortings, the embraces I have wanted. It is my responsibility to tell you who I am as you decide whether to pick me up hold me and take me with you. I would like to believe my failings lovable. In your hands I'm that baby at the next table smearing his face with vegetables.

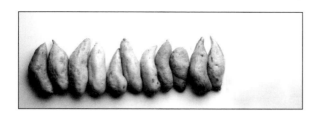

Prince

We were on the leather couch your father gave you, soft and long enough to lie on. How many men sat here with you, taking in your ripe legs, your round knees, how many did more than look. I was holding your small strong hand. We chattered gaily as the teenagers lurched through. Your hands, relaxed demurely on their backs in your lap, lured me when I first saw you, perfectly postured on a camp chair.

When I proposed to you, going to my knees by the bed, putting on your slim finger an emerald you still wear opposite the platinum set that succeeded it, we shared our joy with the son to whom you are closest, but he already knew: Yes, I'm so happy for Mom, there hasn't been a steady man around here since Brian.

I wondered about others when you let me into your twin bed. Your bedroom gave on the tangled yard from which the cat would leap to watch us at the west window.

You're a fast driver. You love to laugh. You say what you think. Or is it what you feel? I can't keep up, the love story curdles in my head.

Maybe that's why I dreamed we were walking down Fifth Avenue towards the Museum of Modern Art on our first date, and I was tired from my work in the office above the atrium and feeling I deserved to be tired. But you were excited to be on the Avenue with me, stimulated by the hustle and bustle oppressing me, and you kept talking until you noticed my lassitude. After a pause to hear about my weariness you resumed, tried to lure me to your enthusiasm, but the crowds and the traffic muffled your words; too much effort to stay abreast, I let your hand go and fell behind, knowing you would be miffed by my losing contact, nursing my self-righteousness as a vast black square Hummer slammed into the crowd, wiping the sidewalk clean of people before the steps of St. Thomas Cathedral, whose traditional services I have for decades longed to attend in memory of my language-rich adolescence at boarding school. Into the sidewalk clean but for gum-spots fell a toothless bum whose pink-purple face indicated something inside pushing him to the brink of death. Blood spreading on his grimy plaid shirt prevented thumping his heart. The only hope was to breathe into the smelly depths of his lungs through the spumey yellow of his mouth, and no one in the literal or figurative uniform of a good Samaritan materialized.

Retching I step from the crowd that jostles me with the outrageous force of bodies thirty-deep, hating my sense of obligation to some obscure higher being motivating my benevolence as I remove my tie, hand my jacket to an old lady who clasps it to her drooping bosom, fresh from communicating at Anglican evensong. I bring my face to the bum's face, attach my mouth to his, the sticky moisture establishing a hermetic seal. I blow hard, remembering how strong my lungs are from a youth of swimming and wrestling and a middle-age of jogging, and while my mouth is working his mouth my nose is enduring a stench worse than any subway bathroom. He's beginning to twitch; his yellow crusty eyes open wide, focus on me, and during my next powerful breath into his gummy hole he throws his arms around my neck, thrusts his tongue into my mouth, twitching, and groaning in pleasure. He slides his body under mine and grasps me with his legs. I am too weak to detach myself from his pleasures, and presently he threatens to wrestle me to my back, where my limp nakedness will be exposed and abused before the evening rush hour crowd on Fifth Avenue. The old lady steps forward and yells "Heal" in a booming voice that summons two policemen and an ambulance crew, who because my starched white shirt is covered with blood and dirt do not know if they should rescue me or the bum or both, but because the bum is yelling in Australian intonation that just because I gave him a dollar that doesn't give me the right to take liberties they let him go and strap me to a stretcher despite my outrage and my business card. No one in the crowd will attest to my good character and my good deed. They attach an IV near my bicep in the ambulance.

I wake late the next afternoon, feeling hung over. My bed gives on a view of the harbor I am amazed a hospital can afford in a Manhattan run by relentlessly competing developers.

You are ecstatic, you've never seen such a total panorama of the harbor, and while I think about Stephen Crane's sky and the pollution producing the pinks and purples of the sunset, the dirty water, the chemical plants in Jersey, the hands that led me to you caress my cheek, smooth my hair, remove my IV, give me clothing that is big and floppy on me. I roll up the pantslegs and the sleeves and you say, "Hey cool, great look." You open the window, persuade the window-washer to give us a ride down on his platform, and your laughter while I grip the ropes and avert my eyes from the view above below and around is music that a string quartet plays on the concrete esplanade for the rush-hour crowds, and once again I can love the big city.

I have never broken a bone, never suffered debilitating disease. It has been decades since I've experienced financial insecurity.

Whenever you look angry my heart sinks, all grace of speech and motion leaves me.

You are 5'7" and weigh 140. I have bench-pressed you. If we fought I could hurt or immobilize you in seconds. You have never threatened me physical harm.

The Prince of Wales endeared himself to me by writing his lover he longed to be a unit of Tampax inside her.

I am of the crowd that loves a lover.

His princess was alive when Prince of Wales sought to pick you up. He'd completed a polo match. Famous actors and rock stars watched. The pinkness of his pale royal complexion, the hints of perspiration at his temples were dramatic in the Florida sun. He jumped from the tons of lethal animal he had controlled through perilous jostlings to ask you if the match was a pleasure for you.

Heads turned. You are blond. You are so lively that friends of your children have made passes at you.

I pursued you so assiduously by car, phone, letter that one evening when you asked me not to come by, hinting another man would be there, I cried in your passenger seat. When we first kissed you closed your eyes and followed my receding face with a sigh, as if

I was breathing you in. It was dark, and we were on a bridge across the rushing stream that confounded Ichabod Crane. We could see the bright foam where rocks speeded the waters. You love the word "romantic." I smitten by everything you touched, even your car, which your son had backed into a fire hydrant, denting the center of the trunk with a vertical crease, so that I could pat its big grey ass.

You continued home to your father's condo, while the Prince of Wales retreated, mallet on his shoulder, across the vivid turf his huge steed paused now and then to crop, and rejoined the crowd.

Jack's Ladder

Jack drove along the waterfront. To the left tourist spots like the aquarium and the cinema showing the eruption of Mt. St. Helen's in three dimensions, to his right the viaduct under which he would look for parking and the club with the twenty large screens where he was to meet the guys. He felt vague about which guys. Pedestrians gesticulated at him; a big stubble-faced bloke came at him from the center of the road. Jack kept the window up, but when the derelict stopped by his front hood, leaned down and shook his head, Jack caught the meaning of the hubbub: he had a flat.

Yeah, he'd whacked a curb making a righthand turn too tight in Capitol Hill. But *fuck* this new expensive car with its gas-eating wide wheels. Why did he let her persuade him to spend all that money? All he wanted was something he could get up and go in, not a computer on wheels.

Jack needed five tries to get the trunk open with the fucking remote. He hefted the 23 ballbreaking boxes of quarry tile she'd made him return. Dammit he'd forgotten, their weight running up his gas-use for weeks.

The doughnut felt light after the tile pile. He leaned it against the black plastic strip that passed for a fender, cursed the scrapes on it, and tried to remember how much *The Consumer Report* said the useless suckers cost to replace after you tapped something. The jack looked big enough to lift a plate of cookies; it was painted metallic gray to match his car; a fucking designer jack. The jack-hole on the frame behind the front wheel was so tiny he couldn't feel it, he had to get onto his back to find it. He forgot to loosen the nuts, so he had to drop it and lift it again, and the jack tilted a little towards the rear, but it was back up and he went for the doughnut but it was gone. He'd heard a monster truck grind by, maybe the goddam rednecks grabbed his doughnut—he ran where he thought the truck had gone. A bunch of rednecks with beerbottle in big trucks grinned at him. He wanted to start something but there were too many of them. They roared with laughter yelling, "Good job, Jack!" as he turned to watch the Vovo roll backwards off the jack and onto the fucking tiles. He felt the dirty water on his new cream slacks and the back of his new cream sweater cooling.

The guys were mostly guys from his business, salesmen who cracked up congratulating him on what a good job he was doing with his errands for the little woman. They annoyed him so much he got as drunk as he could but still drive back to the East Side. His favorite middleweight lost a bum decision in New Jersey.

Jack was so angry at home that night, and so stubborn the next morning in front of his young son that his wife filed for divorce that afternoon and forced him from the house that night.

Jack sold medical supplies all over the state, so he was

accustomed to living on his own, and he didn't give a shit about the money or his home or anything, so he headed out the door on an anger high that beat the hell out of life sitting around with the bitch hearing what she'd bought and her plans for renovating the next bathroom.

The fucking hotel was way across a mall the size of Spokane. He felt like an asshole walking the four-lane boulevard on the curb--of course there was no sidewalk in these expensive suburbs built for expensive cars--and then like an asshole on display as he walked the near-empty parking lot lit up like a football stadium. He couldn't remember why he didn't take the car.

The cable tv was out in the whole fucking hotel, the bar was closed, so he took a hot shower for 20 minutes trying to use up all their hot water, and then all there was to do was read the tourist guide and the Gideon's Bible. The tourist guide catalogued the shops in the mall.

His doorbell rang. It was that tall blond on television all the time, the It Girl. Her face was nothing, kind of a horseface, but her body was amazing and as she and her camera crew streamed past him he reminded himself to look up the video of her doing it on the internet now he was a free man. They were shooting an ad called "There's a Lot of Sherry in the Sheraton," in which she tripped moist and naked through billowing steam from the shower of an average-Joe guest, which had to be Jack because he was the only non-uniformed guest in a hotel filled with flight crews and attendants. "This is your lucky night, man."

The camera crew was all over the room with their blinding lights and blinding reflectors as Sherry Sheraton dropped her scanty clothes onto the foot of Jack's bed, and talked to the director about the blocking as if her bush and her tits were her normal outfit. She murmured "Umm, nice one," when Jack's towel slipped. They put Jack back to bed.

It was a wrap after the 23 takes: they got the back edge of tit, the jut of hip right, no ass to call down the FCC. They liked the contrast of his hairy, droopy body with Sherry's sleek perfections. Sherry was all sympathy about his divorce. "Now you need a little fun," she crooned in a voice airy and pouty.

Jack's wife was smooth as a fish when they were first together, but now she was more like one of those cuts of meat you send back to the butcher for more slicing because it's ringed by white fat you don't want to pay for.

Sherry stood, her tongue in the corner of her moist lips. "You know what I live for, Jack? —Guys like you that appreciate me. People think all I want is stars and hunks: I've had them all, and they're *bore-ring*. I want a guy to pant like a dog for me; I want him to experience the miracle." She bumped and ground, guiding Jack's hands to everything he could want. Her tongue was soft on his fingers as she took his hand in her teeth; her breath was a soothing warmth, smelling of herbed meat. Her breasts were alive under his palm like sleek animals, the taut sections of her ass delicious predators.

As he took his first kiss from the lips and the tongue that suggested the moist soft warm flesh between the sinuous thighs towards which his stiff member was impelled like a crazed engine, he sensed the slightly stale odor his wife took on when excited, an odor that had always made him feel he was missing something.

The crowbar of his member became kielbasa and then rigatoni

beneath the agitations of Sherry's long, delicate fingers, and as she crooned *wussamatter big-guy, you need a little frenching down there* he wrestled himself from her encircling limbs and rose from the bed. Sherry lay back spread eagled and then kicked his hip, "Come *on* you common tacky little bastard." and he felt paralyzed, as if she had dislocated his thigh.

He was afraid, not of the pain but of the bulbs on the front porch dying if he didn't repot them after winter storage, and the black-brown of the potting soil reminded him of his wife's

But now the alarm was ringing even though it was Saturday. The bed was warm where his wife had slept; he would never tell her or the therapist about the dream. What he liked about the therapy was how much smarter it made him, how it helped him answer the question how he could go on living with their son dead. The answer was that he didn't know, but he could or was it should. Nothing could touch the grief that hit them like a kick in the stomach and took their life away. The fumbling attempts of their friends to bring everything back to normal or to imply their son's killing himself was somehow for the better because if he'd do that he didn't fit made Jack want to follow his son, but working with Leah in therapy he managed some sympathy for their friends' obtuseness. Jack knew that his son's madness put the boy outside anything the neighbors could deal with and he sympathized because there were so many times when it seemed beyond anything he and his wife could live through. He remembered when pregnancy had seemed like that, and then how the tiredness of working when the baby wouldn't sleep, the fear when the little thing got sick were insurmountable troubles they got through. But he never felt good about how he got through the earlier crises until his son died; it was not the crappy sentiment that his son's death had meaning, he would never ever accept his illness and death; it was that his own life seemed almost coherent now that he could try to talk about it with the woman with whom he'd lived for 20 years.

She appeared with eggs the way he loved them. The smell of eggs was sexy, and he began to hope because she was still in her bathrobe. Desire started as a tingling ache in his penis, and a wish that she would make the first move. He was never sure if she wanted it, sometimes he was convinced, but then when he touched her she was surprised.

"Yes, I'm awake. I'm lying here thinking. You know what I'm thinking."

"What're you thinking, dear?"

"I'm thinking eggs are sexy."

"Well-well."

"No see, they're smooth and soft like right here."

He traced the lines between her breasts with his thumb and forefinger as she handed him the tray. He pulled her to him for a kiss, but she held back.

"Wait honey, I haven't brushed my teeth yet. Either have you." He wished that just one time they could just drop everything and do it. The ache in his penis wanted instant soothing, petting, mothering.

"You finish those sexy eggs while I get beautiful."

He was so grateful she took his desire seriously that he wept. It amazed him, particularly since the death, when anyone was earnest about what he needed. It amazed him that he could sleep late and his wife who regularly woke so early and was usually tired by early afternoon could cheerfully accede to his desires—hey, he was getting smart, "accede to his desires" was pretty good.

"Honey," he said when she came in just the way he liked her, the

robe gone, her knees showing below the nightgown, "you know what you're doing?—You're acceding to my desires."

"No I'm not, you're acceding to mine. Do you know what you were doing to me while you were asleep last night?"

Jesus, he thought.

"You were caressing my bottom and asking me for my little flower-pot. It was so cute. I almost woke you up and, well, you know."

Later after therapy—where in six months they had never once discussed sex—they took a walk, through the light rain. She wanted to, he didn't because she walked slowly and examined everyone's gardens. He wanted a walk to be a walk, so his cardio-vascular system would benefit. But he knew it would not be the end of him to compromise, and maybe if they kept doing these walks he'd begin to remember the names of flowers and trees. Also, he would practice talking to her before the next walk, maybe asking that they walk faster every other time. He hoped he could do the talking. It occurred to him, though he shied from the connection, that he could walk slow this time because he'd gotten what he wanted.

His wife was 52. She was 5'5" and weighed 149, facts she lamented but to which he was indifferent. He noticed the cellulite when she was standing; when she lay down naked the puckers and bumps smoothed and her body composed itself into what he wanted. He watched her back bent forward, the stooping of her shoulders, and the slowing of her walk; he loved her aging declining being. The testiness that came with her menopause weighed on him, but he withdrew when she berated him. When their son died she overate; she was unpredictably cranky; worst of all, she fell into days which seemed like weeks of silence and silent crying. He hated it when she was immobilized; he felt left out when she was too depressed to function, and jealous that she got to show more emotion than

60

he: it was his son too, so why couldn't he be given a stage on which to grieve? His grief hit him at odd moments like driving, when he was alone in the house, or entering a prospect's lobby.

The therapist once asked him why he was not looking at his wife, and directed him to look at her. Jack was overwhelmed.

"What are you feeling?"

"I'm feeling judged."

"Can you talk about it?"

"No it's hopeless. What I feel doesn't matter."

"You're very sad. Is it your son?"

"Yes, of course, but it's also her, I don't know how to talk about myself with her. I've spent too long trying to please her. I thought that's what men do."

"Lots of men think that. We men are not very smart."

After that session they had the worst fight they could remember. She would not let go of his insult: how could he feel that she was not on his side, how could he? He slept in the guest room, happy that the fucking marriage was over, and now he could live his life the way he wanted to.

The next morning he saw her shoulders stooping over the sink, and he told her he was sorry.

Her illnesses annoyed him. She used chemical fertilizers and pesticides, oblivious to the environment and the cancers they could cause in her. He imagined her dying a long expensive death, slowly wearing him down as she died hideously disfigured, and he blamed her for not taking care of herself. When she caught colds or suffered from the flu she stayed too active for her own good, and he was annoyed she didn't follow his prescriptions for recovery. He had imagined her submissively kind when they met; he had imagined a woman the opposite of his harsh mother.

He experienced her deviations from his expectations as a harsh insult. He kept track of the insults. It could be a nightmare to be with the woman he loved, especially because he knew most of the time that the nightmare was his invention.

Towards the end of the walk they ran into a colleague of his from work.

"Hey, Jack and Leah, come on in, we're just having dessert and Madeira. We were talking about you guys. Come on in. Don't bother with your shoes, we're cleaning tomorrow."

He was so insistent they couldn't say no. All the neighbors fussed over them, no matter what their relationship had been before.

The dessert was a plum pudding Jack knew they'd gotten at the expensive specialty shop, a pudding his wife found irresistible. Soon she was asking for seconds as they discussed the pros and cons of an initiative to lower the gas tax. His hosts were all for dropping any tax on anything, but Jack and his wife were not so sure. It always seemed like folks were getting huffy over a few cents or dollars a month. His wife had three servings of the pudding, Jack two, and they both had too much Madeira. Their bellies hurt and they had to pee when they left. His wife couldn't make it, and Jack stood guard as she crept into a particularly pompous set of terraced hedgerows.

"Good fertilizer, honey."

"Actually it burns the roots."

"Well, their dog comes after our plantings, so this is payback. And they get the sweetest pee around."

"Oh, Jack, you're so cute. I love you."

When she lay down naked, and as the cellulite on her buttocks composed itself he wished he could get rid of the pock-marks on his back from the pimples he still got when he ate too much sugar. He didn't mind the scar from the excised ganglion, but it shamed him to sprout pimples in his 50's and once again, as he climbed onto her buttocks to rub her shoulders and lower back, soothing her into sleep he prayed would last more than five hours, he resolved to give up all the foods and lattes and cocktails that disfigured his back and distended his belly. Sometimes he was bitter that she never massaged him unless he begged, he wanted her to come at him like a mother anticipating his needs, needs she met more fully than anything on earth, would they ever stop rising in him anew and eluding, like his thoughts, the peace he could feel when he hid his face in her lap and wept under her soft touch.

Robin Hood
and the Virgin

for Toby Olson

Mrs. Young wept as she accepted her bouquet from Ashley Reid, who smirked through her curtsey. I caused the tears.

I was alone downstage, rubbing my bow. I was sitting on a stump deep in the woods, hiding from authority. Musing on my bow, my solitude, and everybody wronging and pursuing me, I strained to hold my face intent, but the crescendo of demands from the crowd rattled me. "Hey, Lou, what's happening? Hey, Lou, what's going on? Hey Lou. Hey Lou. Lou. Lou. Lou. Big Lou! Looge! Looge! Lou! Lou! Lou!" I kept on rubbing, but they caught me when I stole a glance across the lights, "Yeah, Lou. What the heck. Comeon Lou DO SOMETHING!"

Maid Marion appeared, arms waving to pantomime struggles through thickets, then opening wide to the joy of stumbling on me in the bright clearing.

"Robin Hood!"

"Maid Marion!"

We raced to each other, stopping a pace shy with arms outstretched, to be certain it was indeed us. We'd been through so much.

"Robin Hood!"

"Maid Marion!"

We moved tight, eager arms falling limp, noses inches short of the kiss we couldn't do in the sixth grade.

"Robin Hood!"

"Maid Marion!

The audience howled and hooted. We fumbled our lines for the rest of the play.

I'd disguised myself in a purple shirt. Unbuttoning in the infirmary behind backstage, I heard gasps, and the school nurse was berating me and guarding The Maid, Camilla McCaslin, who shielded her smooth white chest behind a yellow-tasseled sun hat.

She needed the time I mused on the stump to recover. So did I: I "liked" Camilla.

I had no ambition to be Robin Hood, but I found myself projecting loud and deep auditioning to be Little John, a simple part with few lines for which my girth qualified me, and the my mysterious enthusiasm foisted the lead on me.

All I remember of the remaining brain-racking scenes is the Sheriff Kenny Patrick with his pencil mustache yelling, "Seize him, men!" while Mitch Howe who got Little John supported me with whispered lines.

Next year's drama was the Christmas pageant, and Mrs. Young banished every onstage boy from "Robin Hood" to the stage-crew. We welcomed our exile. We flicked spit wads at the actors while they rehearsed. We played cards, wrestled, and made cutting remarks about players. This was the seventh grade, and the urge to be bad consumed us.

"Good old BK"—Billy Kingman--manned the control and lighting panels. Once a month he projected movies from the California Spanish balcony in his darkened living room while we conducted mad make-out parties on the floors and sofas. His parents were great too, staying out of the way until the lights returned and we were smoothing our clothes to hide the ripples of our orgy. None of us made out, but we exclaimed in enough detail over what we'd gotten off this or that girl to satisfy ourselves. We ate gobs of snackfoods prohibited by most parents, drank rivers of pop, belched, and launched scurrilous remarks at the girls, who clustered in giggling huddles.

BK reported directly to the stage manager, the freckled Ashley Reid, who carried a clipboard at all times. We despised Ashley for her grades, her freckles, her neat clothing, her relentless competence, and her English father.

The modest buildings of Bethlehem had been painted onto a scrim in art class. Floodlights penetrated the scrim to illuminate indoor scenes. Mrs. Young, whose dramatic passion, long straight gray hair, and tears over each year's failure rendered her pathetic, shared direction of the pageant with Mrs. Bianchi the chorus teacher, a tall solid woman we called Horseface. Mrs. Bianchi articulated lyrics and lines so emphatically that the demonstrative movements of her large mouth, a toothy cavern in a pronounced jaw, made her seem all lips, teeth and tongue below her double shiny black buns.

Mrs. Young urged us toward gestures and expressions of feeling for which we had no inner equipment. Nor could we care about ancient foreigners across the Atlantic. But Horseface knew how to do it: the docile girls' choir singing hymns, sanctimonious readers from garlanded folders, silent actors in familiar tableaus.

The stage-crew had plans for the big afternoon of the premier: we dispatched the wildest member of our gang, Sexy Lex, to befuddle BK into giggles.

And so the revelation of the manger was played with the lights on, not through, the scrim. The audience gazed for long minutes at a burlap town of Bethlehem. From behind the scrim issued occasional foot-scrapings and casual murmurs.

BK yelled "Holy shit!" and performed fits of rapid switching. Bethlehem underwent a kaleidoscope of colors, and selected buildings, the stage-floor, the curtains and the audience were spotlighted. The instant BK's lights found the holy family we chopped off the scene. The plunging curtain slapped the stage loudly and puddled towards the audience.

Then we yanked the curtains high exposing kings and magi scurrying to positions of devotion to Camilla the Virgin adoring her ceramic child. While each gesture by the holy family and their adoring visitors stimulated paroxysms of song from Horseface's girls, we sent our genuine German Shuco windup racing-cars whizzing by the Virgin's feet as rodents and poultry must have scurried about the ur-manger.

We tolerated our classroom teachers, despite their social inferiority. But teachers enthusiastic about their subjects like Mrs. Young lost our esteem, which we reserved for sports coaches and the handful whose ineluctable discipline scared us. So the function of the faculty was to supply targets for the snobbery and prejudice essential to our development. When I say "we," I mean of course upper middle-class whites: us.

After the pageant I felt ready to throw a mad make-out party in my father's mansion, promising everyone hot times in the endless chambers and nooks above and below ground. I promised cool girls from other private schools. The girls in your school are dogs and pigs whose embraces you settle for because only you're horny. I was able to convince Cynthia Courier and Sandra Schaum to come. Cindy was widely-rumored to have slept with a boy—they spent the night in their pajamas in the same bed. We were flabbergasted by her. She was average-looking, but totally cool. Although I'd been taught the facts of life, the most vivid explanation of sex in my head was from a servant's son who told me you put it into the girl and went to sleep. If you happened to "get restless" and pee in your slumbers you'd feel good and make a baby. Sandra Schaum was so good-looking it was scary. She looped black patent-leather belts through her cotton school-uniform dresses: replacing the drab cloth sash made a statement no other girl dared match. The identical initials of these girls' first and last names confirmed their coolness, and in triumph I told everyone that "CC" and "SS" would be there.

My father allowed me to turn the lights down low and to play all the rhythm-n-blues 78s I'd collected, even "Work with me, Annie." We danced slow, our arms draped about each others' shoulders and upper backs, staggering in clinches we'd never get off the girls were there no hot music playing. Sandy gave me a big smile and buried her face in my neck as we swayed. Startled, I hoped my pals were watching us. I danced close with Cindy. Then I found myself inviting her down to the cellar. She accepted.

I'd spend many hours down there, wandering about and puzzling over the strange objects in the huge arched irregular space: dusty tools used by the staff that had maintained the orchard, the prize-chicken coop, the riding-horses and carts, and the acres of gardens. There were rows of English saddles and harnesses under dust. I read illustrated editions of Sir Walter Scott in the paneled library, and I sought to be moved and to make these discarded implements my family heritage.

Down there with Cindy it felt being on stage; a hollow weak being infested my limbs, my voicebox. We chatted a bit, paused and looked at each other. It was time to put out, but I talked faster and pulled down the wood-tined rakes, the scythes, the sledgehammers, the mallets. I demonstrated a pedal-driven grindstone. As I was sharpening a hoe, Cindy left for the "ladies room," and I hung there seeking friendship from these objects of my imagined nostalgia.

Corn, Cones, Conchs

for Bob Lamberton and Bruce Connor

It wasn't much of a pinecone. Half its scales were gone. It was dusty grey-brown. Lying next to gum-wrappers and shredded foil it didn't threaten the earth with reproductive responsibilities. It would soon be vacuumed away by one of those slow big square machines that suck in leaves and any other detritus not sticking or congealing. It might mulch the waters five miles beyond Sandy Hook. It was an evergreen urban victim. But it begins this book, and this book wants to be a love story.

In this book terrible things happen, and the reader should be warned, for the hero and heroine start out weak and troubled, meet, fall in love, fight, hurt each other, get stronger, get weaker, get married, and live. Their names are Louis (loo-iss) and Arianna. People die around them, but they live on and get what they deserve: each other.

I like the hero and I tried to love the heroine. The older I get the more sentimental I become. Writing this book is aging me considerably, for the heroine kept bothering me. She rubbed her crotch against my shoulder as I typed. She was wearing the red bathing suit I bought her. The suit rode up between her thighs, and curlicues of pubic hair, tiny because she'd shaved it off two months ago, peeped at me as I hunched over the keys. And the top liked to ride down, so I could look at her nipples whenever I cared to. Once she got angry and laughed at me when I told her to keep her body in the suit at the beach. Her rubbing her crotch on my shoulders wouldn't have bothered me if it weren't that I was learning to use an electric typewriter. For years I'd punched away at a manual whose keys had turned sticky and grey.

So it was difficult to control my fingers. The space bar would stutter across the page. The hairs were scratchy against my sunburn. I was trying to write a poem, and the poem was for another woman. I was trying to find an echo for "eye." The poem was an acrostic.

My heroine Arianna has soft lips. When she is horny she looks like a little girl asking her daddy for extra hot fudge on her banana split. She puts her thumb and her little finger in her mouth and sucks it. You feel like a child-molester in an ideal state run by Prince Kropotkin and the Divine Marquis.

The obvious rhyme was "thigh" but the poem was on a higher level. Arianna is anything but stupid. She makes me feel stupid and inept. Mostly I like writing about her more than being with her. I tried to keep working. No woman was going to disturb WRITER AT WORK. I WOULD NEVER LET SO MINOR A MATTER AS A

NEAR-NAKED WOMAN DISTRACT ME FROM MY LABOR TO CREATE. I HEARD A SEDUCTIVE GIGGLE BREAK THROUGH THE INSISTENT VOICES OF MY MUSE. DO YOU WANT TO FUCK ME? WHAT? YOU HEARD ME. WELL, DO YOU? DAMN IT I'M WRITING. CAN'T YOU SEE I'M TRYING TO WRITE A DIFFICULT POEM? YEAH, IT'S ABOUT THAT FRECKLE-FACE IRISH NIT, YOU DUMB PENIS. WHY DON'T YOU UNLOCK THE SHIFT KEY?

okitsalousypoemand now youveruineitforme justasyouruineverythingand isulkeduntilshe putherhandhinside.

It's not easy being an author. I tend to jump ahead. We fuck towards the end of the book, in detail, but we fuck all through it in selected episodes. I don't go down on her much, but she blows me often, usually when I'm driving. That usually lasts from 42nd Street along the East River Drive South across the Brooklyn Bridge, along Atlantic Avenue to about Sackett Street on Third Avenue because there is too much traffic on Fourth, the route of the New York Marathon, as I groan and lose control.

But I know you're dying to hear more about the pinecone, and how it was the seedpod, as it were, of all that follows.

Well, Arianna has a large ass. I studied it, knowing that someday it would be my duty to describe it, and that the passage would have to be long. I think I began to study it before we saw the pinecone. Sometimes she wears those designer jeans you pour yourself into but then look like a pitcher or vase, the material is so stiff. When we drove to the beach that day with her son, she wore something softer, and there was no difficulty knowing where to aims ones eyeballs when she walked ahead. But since Arianna, another urban victim, seldom walks, getting behind in the open can be a problem. Then there's the problem of the ass itself. I'm in love with it, and it takes the shapes of the moods in my head. Or it doesn't. It's hardly small, it's soft. Naked I cannot see it clothed, clothed I can't see it naked. Soft, it conforms to what covers it.

As you can see, I get lost. At the beach she wore baggy jeans, no fashion attached: they looked like some man's pants. Maybe they were. Her hair was cutely unkempt, and the wind blew it and her clothes in all directions. Her shoes didn't match her pants, and her shirt didn't match her jacket. He jacket was a light green svelte suede thing. Her hair was straightened, but it stuck up and out like an afro seeking to express itself. It was cold and windy at Riis Park, and as soon as we parked we started moving fast. Arianna ran towards the water; she stumbled, fell and sat in the sand, giggling. She denounced the sand in her shoes and pockets, cursing in front of her little son, who was running happily in circles. She brushed herself off. I offered her a thorough brushing-down. She giggled, as she had the night before.

The night before we were in a hideous restaurant, the Purity. She was drinking Tab with lemon, and removing the bun from her hamburger, leaving grey-brown meat with an oily patina. I was drinking Sanka and getting heartburn. We were on religion. We'd been to a meeting. From an earlier meeting I had a card imprinted with compressed doctrine. I was in a good mood. I pulled the card, rumpled and soiled from a stay in Arianna's purse, from my breast pocket. I affected puzzlement about a few crucial words, including "conscious contact." I held the card next to her plate, soiled paper beside the meat epidemic.

"I think it said. . ." and I leaned over the table, pulling the card back. She leaned over too, acting helpful, putting on seriousness. She didn't understand me, maybe never will.

"It says here. . ." she leaned further, so that I could look into her shirt, or her eyes. I remember her chin and neck: I rate her neck first, shoulders second, ass third, eyes, fourth, breasts fifth. At this moment her eyes (and I expect mine) were flashing, twinkling, scintillating—all those lovely things the eyes and the flesh just about them do when you both know what you really mean but it could spoil the fun to say it. I know what I really meant, haven't a clue what she did. She put her elbows on the table, squeezing her breasts. She had spilled the Tab and soiled her shirt, but I didn't tell her.

At Riis Park, Arianna was giggling and cursing and her son running about and I took her by the shoulders and was stunned by how narrow, how small she was. I couldn't say anything funny or sexy. We couldn't look at each other for these few moments. She stared at my chest, refusing to lift her eyes. I let go and ran after her boy. She caught up to us at the boardwalk.

"Let's go the playground."—We both said it at once. We giggled, happily embarrassed. We'd let it out. We couldn't look at each other. I could hardly walk, and couldn't speak.

Along the sandy sidewalk towards the half-destroyed playground. Through the aisle of scrub pines. Over that ochre mix of soil and sand that looks like silt and nightsoil, urban earth. Wrappers, cups, straws, oily spots. Arianna ran a few steps and bent to pick something up. It was two-thirds of a pinecone.

"Look!"

She held it up for her son.

"Look at the lovely acorn!"

I thought I was in love. . . . . .

-2-

It wasn't the first time I was wrong: I had been married before.

Arianna and I got married and she forgot to bring her diaphragm on the honeymoon. Except she didn't forget. She called my ejaculate "sperm-juice" and she was disgusted by it. Disgusted by it and its slime and its redolence of the body. Disgusted also by the idea of its going into the right place: she liked it sprayed like body-lotion all over her.

You can see that the evidence I had for this marriage was less than systematic: I had been infatuated; she was amusingly ignorant; she could be sexy; she tested my patience with her aggressiveness; she had a son; she wanted to get married; she was moody, selfish and lively. I still search my memory of the sixteen months we knew each other before our honeymoon for other reasons to marry.

There were at least two problems with doing it with a diaphragm: she had to put it in, and though she was dexterous in many ways, particularly with a steering-wheel, she had trouble folding that resilient disk and putting it in place: she'd lose patience, ask me to do it; threaten not to have sex; drop it, curse it.

The other problem was that she'd *promised* me she'd use it; she knew that I'd be happier in many ways, local and general. So she forgot it.

And so as newlyweds we were using condoms. If life is a series of hurdles jumped, skirted, bowled over, her vagina was a high, high hurdle for me and for us. I couldn't be clear about this then; her moods and ways were so mercurial; I was beginning to know I could have feelings, and I couldn't keep up with her. I did know sex was a problem for us: we'd gone to a therapist and ignored his suggestions. I also knew that to Arianna the problem for her vagina was my penis: that seldom-happy bit of flesh and veins was asked by her and by me to take pressures it was not built for and not intended to take. And when it couldn't take them, it was wrong, hanging there in shame and pain.

Have you ever wanted to impress someone? You talk and talk and they sense your efforts, remain remote, withdraw affect, and become preoccupied with anything but your efforts. If acknowledged, the efforts are annoying, pesky, tacky, over-earnest, and irrelevant. Well, that was the life my penis led: God I'd try this and try that, I'd do wonderful loving things to her face, neck, shoulders, breast, ass, legs—there was little I missed with hands, lips, tongue, legs. She'd reciprocate with an abrupt pat or rub or two—usually the rub was on my penis and it hurt. She had large strong hands. Then we were ready to do it: I was feeling she was impatient to get it over with, and feeling the need to try: after all this was sex, life's miracle and elixir. But though sore from physical and moral pressure, my penis felt as if it had a lump inside, kind of like a wire in a mannequin holding it ready, but letting it recede a bit from where it was earlier when it had been eager for fun.

So I'd take this sore foreign object and aim it at the entrance to her vagina; or she would. But she was rarely wet or distended, so my thing had to batter or push its way in. This hurt too. Sometimes it gave up, went limp. By now it was no longer in pain, it was numb with that feeling we get when a limb "goes to sleep". Maybe right in the tip there was a trace of vestigial pleasure, enough to cause a quick eventless ejaculation into her hand, her harsh pubic hair, a condom or—oh most rare—her.

Anyway during whatever time I was on top of or inside her, she'd look away, usually to her right, and although she wasn't in pain, she was angry and preoccupied with her own anger. For she felt that sex is something you do one way: right up the middle with the man on top, and she demanded that I do it the right way, but she got little or no pleasure from anything except knowing that we were doing sex the way she said you do it. The condoms helped the unwelcome entry problem: I bought the wet kind, and they made her less unreceptive.

So moving up and down on top of her, looking at her averted angry face for signs of pleasure or response was like telemarketing to hostile prospects. There I was, stuck on one of life's hurdles. Her head dangled back from the honeymoon bed. I hoped it was passion that put her there looking at the room reversed. She always kept her eyes wide open, as if on guard against any stray caresses while doing it.

When I met Arianna I was back from suicide-attempts. We were outpatients in aftercare; we met at my first session outside the hospital. She had been in recovery for two years.

She asked me out after the first meeting. I wasn't ready; I refused her company and her ride back to the hospital. I could walk myself, dammit.

It was my road back from death to drop that "dammit," and it never did occur to me that I could indeed walk by myself, that self mattering so little.

During the honeymoon a condom broke. I'd not learned to squeeze the air from their tips, and my idea of what you do in there may have been a little rough, a notion of "giving it to her." So the aftermath of the across-the-bed, head-hanging honeymoon fuck was panic, "My life was ruined when I got pregnant before. I don't want to get pregnant. You call the doctor, Louis; you can get the doctor right now please. I'm embarrassed to. The man should do it. Call him now, dammit. You've had your fun."

I called. The doctor was a charming Italian who delivered our daughter years later, prescribing the pills that addicted Arianna. He found us amusing in our ignorance, and he taught me how to use a condom on my honeymoon.

The waters of this idyll were filled with live conchs. I'd known polished conchs as shelf-pieces in houses in suburbia paradoxically decorated with beach motifs. I'd also "listened" to the shells, as a credulous child and as an adult vaguely aware of things happening in the blood in my ears. I knew that Triton blew one. But here were these shells walking across the floor of the reasonably-clean waters of Polo Isle.

We'd go out to the beach now and then on the honeymoon. Arianna hated to be outdoors and to be active—the things I loved. She'd lie restlessly on a hotel towel on the white sands of brochure vintage, while I swam, trying to enjoy my activity despite her suspicions of it. Truly urban, she'd never learned to swim. When she was pregnant with our daughter she tried to learn. She was happiest telephoning, shopping, and eating.

I saw these touristitem shells walking across the floor of our honeymoon sea. Amazing. It was like my private rendition of "The Lobster Quadrille". I checked my local nature lore by the hotel-room's headstand: these were Fighting Conchs. And they were: you'd dive down near them and they'd assume wonderful defensive postures, claws deployed at you. They were smoothly-dancing houses, little Guggenheim Museums with claws. I wanted to write. They bored Arianna.

Ever since I was little I've spent lots of time swimming under water. Have you ever seen Bruce Connor's short film, "Movie?" It's clips of stock footage of disasters, intercut with a diver exploring a sunken wreck, set to "The Pines of Rome"—lush music by a fascist—and the undersea flora growing from the wreck sway to it as the lone diver pokes around. He moves slowly about the encrusted wreckage, so far away you hope, the only refuge you feel, from the stock images of fires, ruins, famine, oppression—"the air of atrocity/ common/ as a president." He gets deeper and the screen gets darker as the pictures become less comic in their accumulating misery, and you see one child's whole body twitching with hunger and disease—and the loud music moving to its climactic crescendo, and the tiny diver disappears into the submarine wreck.

I hope Bruce Connor is alive. One of my false starts was managing the Film-Makers" Cinematheque, then on 42nd Street, for two days. I'm not complaining, but it's not easy being an author.

The Accounting: a Mystery

for Randy Polumbo

-1-

The cat nuzzled her leg, first she felt the whiskers, then the jawline, and as it pushed, the teeth. The cat's purrs got her hopes up, until it pushed so hard she might as well have been furniture.

The familiar knock: good old Bob. He took her shoulders and kissed her so hard their teeth hit. His hand moved up her thigh as they drove—taking it away for the sharp turn through the stream of traffic defining the mall, to start anew at her smooth knee. It was a hot midsummer night; she wore as little as she could. She hated to perspire in public. The air conditioning at the Little Italian would hit her skin like a cold martini hitting her chest cavity.

Bob was good old Bob because he pursued her doggedly from the day they met. He was balding, and polished his pate. His beard was dark and rose every six hours to resemble magnetized iron filings. He tried a mustache once, but looked like the famous serial killer who doubled as the pillar of a fundamentalist Midwestern church. She had two inches on Bob, and wore flats with him, though she loved what high heels did for her legs and profile as she passed picture windows. He took care to dress in the kinds of clothes she liked, and in their three years together she'd prodded him to replace most of his wardrobe. Bob's eyes were brown; from his chin hung a pouch soft like his body that was strong but seemed without muscles. His back was dark with hair. She loved to pet and stroke him there. She never ceased to be startled by the size and redness of his genitals.

She was an accountant. After college she decided a number of things: she would enter a profession that was open to women, that was fulfilling, but which she would not need to bring home every night; she would go to bed only with men about whom she was serious, never men from work; she would live in a suburb near the big city, where she could afford a luxury condo; she would join a health club; she would travel outside the country alone or with girlfriends; she would invest carefully. She acted on each of these decisions, and the only unexpected events in her life were the arrival of the cat and her relationship with a bald man.

The cat arrived when her best friend died suddenly at the health club. They were running on the treadmills with a view of the City across the Meadowlands, following as always synchronized cardio programs. Suddenly the friend was flung backward from the track, to lie splayed and twisted like a neglected doll, her eyes and mouth wide open. The friend's mother, who looked like a hardened version of her daughter, and who seemed to live at the club, insisted the accountant take the cat as a memory and a token. Her other child, a professional athlete, was too rootless to care for the animal.

Occasionally the cat attacked her, and she shut it in the laundry-room. She kept a tennis racket on her dining-table to ward it off, and never let it into the bedroom.

Her late friend had been surprised by her "settling for" Bob: "Hey, you're too good-looking for a guy who looks like a primate actuary."

But Bob was a famous trial lawyer—the "Mouth of the Mob", in the print and video tabloids. She was ignorant of his fame when they met on a nature-hike near the Shawangunks.

The Little Italian was owned by one of Bob's clients, but he never presumed on the relationship, settling for whatever table the headwaiter suggested. He too had resolved to leave work at the office. They shared the feelings their work elicited, the stresses. and their problem-solving techniques, never the facts of his cases.

Meat lay heavy in the accountant; she ate it only at Bob's urging, and she picked at it as he complained about his expanding practice.

"Why can't you say you're too busy?"

"If you do what they want they trust you. Refusing cases wouldn't be doing what they want. They never want to hear about your problems."

"I see. It's like sewing up a sector. It's a great strategy, but it takes work."

"Yeah, it's like that.—like the way you get all the money manager accounts. That's great business. Loads of money floating around."

"Yeah, they're swimming in it. Doesn't get any better. But you know, Bob, I'd never trust those guys with my portfolio. They charge fat fees, they live the good life, they're exciting, but they don't know the first thing about managing their business. When the market's up they hire people, when it's down they lay them off. They never know where they stand financially. All they care about is the ten-year future and the put/call ratio as a negative indicator."

"Yeah, I'm glad we're not like that."

"Yeah, Bob, I'd hate to lay you off."

"Hey, Babe, you think I'm a drag on your bottom line?"

"No, honey I think you're in the asset column."

And they touched glasses.

He was proud. He was proud to look across the table at a woman whose blond hair was utterly convincing, whose neck was graceful, and whose tan was natural right down to the lines inside her clothes where her skin went white-pink. Visions of pink flesh floated in his head as he gulped and chewed. But it was her bones and muscles that excited him as he gazed at her across his osso buco: the cleft between her collarbone and the SCM muscles that topped the scaffolding of her shoulders.

He grinned at her confident use of trade jargon. He loved earning her total compensation times seven, for he felt that when he asked her to marry him one of these years—that was the closest they got to discussing it, "Hey, we ought to tie the knot one of these years"—he would be attractive to other women if she rejected him and blew their thing away. He was in no hurry: he hated her cat. He'd be happy to dump it into the swamp bubbling behind her high-rise.

Meanwhile the sex was great; it was weirdly exciting that her muscles were defined and his were insulated. Neither was bothered when the other cried out someone else's name at heated moments. It brought them closer, allowing them to share about past relationships.

The nausea from her greasy lamb shanks disappeared when Bob's hand stole back to her thigh under the table. They decided to skip the movie because she had an early plane to Chicago.

As she crept out at 5:00 AM, Bob looked like a hairy troll drooling onto her pink silk sheets.

Her practice had spread from the greater metropolis to Chicago, where she took Milton's Mob—hyper-aggressive hedge fund traders named for their monetarist patron saint at the University—by storm. She gained their accounts, nay, the virtual management of their treasuries by confronting them with their financial management lapses dressed in business suits that ended abruptly in miniskirts. They called her Numberbabe, and were dumbfounded when their wining, dining, their skyboxes, sports cars and private jets failed to seduce her. The young president of a fund whose results surfed the crashing waves of the markets without a spill would not take no for an answer.

He combed his full glistening hair straight back. His perfect tan was real, and his arms and shoulders were elegantly sinewy, not grossly clotted with muscle. He worked out at the East Bank club, where they had their first (she hesitated to call it) date, playing tennis, jogging, and eating health foods including chewy game-meats washed down by his private-label microbrew. The East Bank Club, the planet's most elaborate facility outside the United Arab Emirates, sports the unofficial motto, *If you don't have a good body, you'd better drive one.* Thirty tennis courts, four Olympic-size pools, a quarter-mile track looping around picture-windows behind which rank upon rank of perfect bodies in spandex lifted, danced, and inserted themselves into machines—all under one formerly-industrial roof. As she wondered why she'd settled for dependable Bob, with his fatted-seal body, the young president's eyes swung from a pert ass passing their booth to her own breasts in the tennis jumper—"Hey, Numberwoman, you're the hottest thing going here. Come to my yacht tonight."

"Nope, you keep forgetting I'm here on business."

"Yeah, you make me forget. Why don't you?"

"I can't. A woman has to take care of herself."

"Even accountants need some fun."

"You don't need to tell me that."

"Am I offensive, unattractive?"

"No, you're a dreamboat."

"This is weird. No woman says no to me. I'm star here. A guy like me, I take huge risks every day, and I need it bad."

"Listen, honey, do you want me to introduce you to the woman attached to the ass that walked by? Maybe you'll have better luck with her."

"OK, OK. But you know, you're like a sports car that just sits in the garage. I could rev up that engine of yours."

"You're sweet, honey, but I'd better get back to the Ritz."

The young president insisted she experience what his Testarosa could do, blasting her through a loop along the Lake Shore, skidding to halt beyond the dark Amoco tower at the boat basin, where the sounds of wavelets lapping and halyards striking rigging seemed the upbeat rhythms of the life she wanted, but she complimented him on his persistence and insisted he drive her back to the Gold Coast.

These trips exhausted her, and she took to reading true-crime books at hotels and on the planes. She found the Mafia fascinating but disgusting. One quiet night in bed she asked good old Bob about Vincent Patriarcha's Piranha Limited, a loan-sharking crew in Boston that terrorized deadbeats by dipping their arms into tanks of the carnivorous fish. He leapt from the bed screaming, "Why do you want to read that crap? Why can't you read something intelligent? I thought you had a brain. That's crap, do you hear me, CRAP?" He threw the book into the toxic swamp below.

She said yes to the young president on her next trip to Chicago. What wasn't imported teak on the deck and in the hold was imported mahogany. The thrilling luxury of the ambiance made up for his selfish ineptitude between the sheets—or so she told herself as she lay awake swaying in the gentle currents of the lake beside the snoring entrepreneur. He'd interrupted his necessary but sloppy attempts at oral sex to yell, "Come on, baby, you're getting it good good good!"

She'd never slept on the water, never set foot in a yacht. The rhythmic movements of the deflected tides from the great lake fused her unsettled senses and her imagination: she realized that Bob and the young president were stepping-stones toward a new life incorporating trendiness and Manhattan, a good life that would exclude both men.

One Indian summer morning so bright you could see Michigan she called the young president's private line, groggy despite her tall latte from a private party atop the Hancock Tower. His personal assistant was breathing heavily: "There's been a horrible, horrible tragedy, our leader was murdered on his boat. Haven't you seen the news yet? How can you just casually call like nothing happened!" The accountant wrote the assistant's hostility off to shock. How could the snippy little thing blame her for what after all was a non-exclusive relationship on both sides? Probably she harbored a secret crush on him, despite her hatchet face and her flat figure.

She flipped on the news: her lover's head was mounted on the bowsprit, his torso on the mast, his legs and arms on the rigging. Crows and gulls fought over him. The silhouettes (edited of the scavengers whose cries punctuated the breathless at-the-scene reports) were an unprecedented montage beside the studio portraits of the smiling, even cocky, mogul whose precocity dominated adoring chronicles of his career and glowing reflections on it by executives canny enough to invest in his high-flying funds.

Now Bob's wizardry in bed became overwhelming, his knowledge of her anatomy preternatural. He yelled in horrible but stimulating triumph in response to her cries. She wondered why he screamed out the name of her late workout partner, but relief that passion could still seize her despite the Chicago horror dulled her curiosity. Sexual health was crucial to her.

The Chicago police took control of the case so tenaciously that the FBI, the SEC, and the IRS complained to the media about local hoarding of evidence and leads. Mayor Daley defended his troops, "A rising star in the Chicago economy has been snuffed out prematurely and tragically. I know this is a hot potato, but in Chicago we take the bull by its horns, and we fully intend to get to the bottom of the bloody trail. If we bother anyone by digging aggressively, that's their problem. I shall not rest until the heinious perverted perpetrators are nailed."

Before I purified my life, I gave you the pop-ups on your computer. I was angry with the jocks, the business majors, the frat-boys who scorned me as a nerd. I put a big hairy finger dead center in their computers when they logged in, and laughed myself silly when I heard them grunting and moaning about their screens flipping them the bird. I smoked weekends with my comp sci professor, who saw my talent and treated me like a buddy: we'd giggle about the herd of fools on campus. When I let him in on my little joke he got serious and quizzed me about how I did it. "Wow, man, I think you've onto something big!" The next thing I knew he'd taken a job with the Evil Empire in Medina, Washington. Soon he was a hero in all the computer rags for inventing the new advertising paradigm. He'd stolen my intrusion codes.

And so everything I'd been struggling towards was gone. Why had I been such a good boy, avoiding all the scrapes, all the troubles with drugs and girls and the law "healthy" boys, especially Italian boys, plunge into like surfers into white water? Why had I studied so hard, gotten the academic prizes, the scholarships, why taken such good care of my poor widowed Mom—why, if there was not some payoff? But when I took Asian studies, known to most as "Rice Paddies," for distribution credit, and, beginning to eschew teleological thinking, I realized that the very notion of a payoff, a reward, a prize that could be in any way measured or defined was an illusion. The mantra of the computer world had been *let go of linear thinking.* It remained for me to read Dr. Suzuki and the masters of spiritual being to understand that I needed to let go of linear *living.*

And so I drove my poor mother crazy by refusing offers from Apple and Google, rich offers that would have let me telecommute from our little home in Mahwah, where I cared for Mom, who's never been the same since Dad shot himself two days after coming back from Operation Desert Storm. I arranged for her to join a Merck control group, and the rotating anti-psychotic cocktail held her in check. No longer did she sneak into neighbors' houses to steal their family memorabilia. No longer did she worship in her basement Shrine to the Family, arranging the stolen pictures and trophies with crucifixes, icons, smiling portraits of Pope John, and lighting candle after candle to music by Jerry Vale and Julius La Rosa.

But she continued to scold me for wasting my talents. Flight attendant was my first job out of college: I flew for an airline that would let me see the world, especially the Far East. Then I settled into administrative work for an accountant, "a woman already," as my mother kept saying. My first job gave me more than enough insight into people and cultures. My second job allowed me the peace, I hoped, to perform routine tasks in quiet, earning enough for my simple needs, and enough to complement my mother's always-diminishing retirement benefits from my late dad.

But the Managing Partner of our office insisted on sharing her personal affairs with me. She thought me gay because I was a flight attendant and because I am quiet and gentle. She cannot realize that for me giving up the intoxicating pleasures of the flesh is like giving up meat and dairy products: it takes time to feel the benefits, the serenity and the insights, that a vegetarian spiritual diet provides.

And this chief accountant's story only lends me gratitude for my holy withdrawal. I knew from the start that Bob was a poor choice, and I told her flat out that no number or intensity of orgasms could make up for real affinity. When she fell for the young president, I told her to watch out, for I saw him as a shallow plaything, and I sensed sinister depths in Bob.

I'll never forget her looking at me like a trapped animal, all the self-confidence and all the brashness drained from her as she slumped behind her huge mahogany Partner's desk, wondering if she'd caused her Chicago lover's grizzly death. The perfections of her honed visage and body, her styled clothing blurred and collapsed into the lumpy sobs and wails of an ugly little girl, and my heart went out to her, the foolish heart I'd worked so hard to quell. I resolved to solve what I knew to be double murders—his and her former workout partner's.

"You need a vacation, honey. You just hop a plane to your favorite island, and I'll take care of everything, even that nasty cat."

I studied the file photos of her friend's fatal collapse in the gym. I communed with the images of the victim's mother, with my memories of her. Why was she there with workout clothes identical to the younger women's? I saw a woman approaching the climacteric, driven to overcome nature's inevitable outer decay, the shriveling and decay of the outer layers encasing her spirit. I saw that outer shell hardening, hardening her inside. The signs of cosmetic surgery on her face, neck, arms, buttocks and thighs summoned for me the spirit, nay the demon, of health-club competition run amok. Mother and daughter shared the name Elizabeth, the older using Lizzie, the daughter Betty. I pondered the seeming benevolence of granting the daughter this independence. If the daughter was independent, why was the mother always there in the background, looking like her daughter's decayed future self?

3

Mayor Daley and Chicago's finest were relieved when serial assaults on Muslims in Cicero and South Chicago extracted the media's attention from the Money Master Murder.

Seamus Heaney, a politically-ambitious detective stayed with the case, even though he found it difficult to receive backup from a department that seemed indifferent to a case it so tenaciously protected from the Feds. He reasoned that once he solved it, contributions from the young president's grateful peers would fuel a city council run. Or they could give him consulting work on security, and cut him into investments that could assure the future of his burgeoning Catholic family.

The love angle went nowhere. The detective dismissed the accountant as one of a stream of women making the evening commute from the East Bank Club to the yacht. None of the women was pregnant, or in any way attached to her lover. The only female showing devotion to the young president was his admin assistant, but she lived with her mother and siblings who could account for her whereabouts minute by minute.

That left the business angle. The day before his dismemberment, the president had landed a new private account, but the fund-wire had been voided before the new positions the hedge fund took could settle. According to the portfolio team, voiding an account without notice was unprecedented. They'd hustled for two days to unwind complex market exposures. The placement had occurred directly with the young president, and his notes on it had vanished. Funds had arrived through the Royal Bank of the Cayman

Islands, in the name of a Cayman Islands LLC managing a hedge fund-of-funds whose investment objectives were so vague as to invite SEC scrutiny. The scrutiny had lasted for more than 3 years as teams of New York lawyers fought the watchdog agency over each request for information. The Limited Partners in the fund-of-funds were professional athletes, many of them notorious for hotly-contested suspensions for steroid and stimulant use, their cases handled by the same law firms fighting the SEC. Oddly, the Managing Partners were lawyers and accountants based in the Caymans, not money-managers, and they made it difficult to clarify the fund-of-funds' structure and management by asserting the client confidentiality so respected in Caribbean finance. One Limited Partner, an Italian slugger whose legs would no longer support his squatting behind the plate, was infamous for denying his gay propensities.

The Seamus Heaney retreated from this maze, to hound the South Chicago Imam Mayor Daley denounced on the evening news. The violence against and outrage at Muslims for provoking the attacks with their attire and their suspiciously-complete absence of connections to Islamist terror roiled the Windy City.

-4-

I wore rubber gloves entering her condo. I took care with the small bottle of chloroform. I knew the cat would lash out, and worked with precision in thick clothing to extinguish its senses, not mine. Just as I suspected: a tiny listening device was implanted in the cat's shoulder, in the feline meridians that fuel aggression.

People don't get it about homicide detectives. Some of them think we're real brainiacs like the guys on TV. Some of them think we're dumb bureaucrats who follow routines. This fag who worked for the highfalutin accountant must have thought I was suicidal crazy. He comes in here with a story of a nice cat that's a bad cat because it has a listening device installed by Bobbie Bonanzo who's in cahoots with the murdering mother of that bimbo whose heart stopped in the yuppie gym, and he's sure the mother and Bonanzo are longtime lovers and she's having remote control sex with him by listening in while Bobbie Bonanzo gets it on with her daughter's friend. He's certain that the momma and the daughter both being Elizabeth is a "vital clue." Clue, my ass, you dumb flit. He's sure Bobbie arranged the hit on the Chicago yuppie, but not sure if the murderous mom knows that. "That's where the case stands, right, sir?" the puny excuse for a wop says to me. He wants me to protect him from Bobbie no less, while I contact Chicago's fucking finest.

He'd forgotten to look up the mom's Old Man. There's some things you've just got to know in this world. But I wrote down everything he told me, real slow in pencil to frustrate him because he wanted voice recognition or some shit, and I thanked him and told him he'd be hearing from us. Sure, kid, I'm going to give up a nice living for the pursuit of justice. I started an office pool on whether he'd be dead in one two or three weeks, win, place, show.

-6-

The detective's body language gave him away. Criminals have a way of going still, like a snake about to strike. I remember that from my Uncle Bruno's bar in Mahwah.

I have set up a Crummie Trust for my mother.

Time to spend my frequent-flyer miles.

-7-

It's amazing how little sex connects to what we are thinking and feeling. The accountant suspected that Bob was behind the president's murder and behind her administrative assistant's sudden disappearance. But she could not, would not keep him from her king-size extra-firm mattress. Nor could she question him about her cat's disappearance. She accepted his proposal, and they are raising twin boys in a mc-mansion in Summit. Bob wants them to be Jersey politicians, sending them to the best private schools, to whose endowments he makes substantial contributions. The accountant has sold her practice, keeping busy with the boys, social clubs, charities and a health club.

The Don Juan legend is the story of surviving and thriving in hell. Bob knows more about the grizzly practices and the greasy manipulations of New Jersey's Mafia than anyone on earth. Despair for his soul drives the priapism of this small, hairy man. Early on it drove him into the arms of Elizabetta Montevenero, the ripely mature wife of Enrico (The Jackhammer) Montevenero, who had earned his popular soubriquet not only with violence but also with dazzling success developing gamey landfills into high-end commercial and residential properties. When Bob realized whose favors he was sharing, he dragged Elizabeth and himself back from the abyss, and they substituted perverse schemes of perverse unfulfillment for their elaborate copulations. These schemes included the seduction and then the snuffing, to fulfill Elizabeth's jealous frenzy, of her own daughter by means of a toxic electric dose from her treadmill. The mother had thought she could satisfy her jealousy of her daughter's fresh body by pimping her to Bob. But Bob's crying out her daughter's name, never hers, as his copulations with the accountant came to her via the transmitter in the cat were gall and wormwood. Amphetamines and exercise bulimia pour fuel on the rage Elisabeth will take to her grave. Meanwhile she watches paunchy, perspiring mobsters like her husband bed any bimbo they want.

Bob and Mikie Mont, the famous catcher of dubious sexuality, are the only members of the extended Montevenero family to have suffered financial damage when the hedge fund-of-funds that had wired the money to the young president's company in Chicago collapsed, a collapse forcing the Fed to provide liquidity so several banks based in New Jersey.

Seamus Heaney, disappointed that his year-long unbeaten streak convicting Imams under Patriot Act statutes failed to create a popular groundswell, returned to the cold Money Master Murder case, computer skills enhanced by his cyberwork exploding Muslim charitable fronts. He ran checks on all Limited Partners in the young president's hedge funds. Senior executives from Chicago's huge roster of Fortune 500 enterprises were in. The great Milton Friedman was in.

But what was the family trust of Augusto Pinochet doing there? Did he maintain, even in his harassed dotage, close contact with the great monetarist? Had their connection menaced the young president? You could scarcely call the M.O. of his murder a "disappearance."

Then he dug into the bankrupt fund-of-funds whose phantom contribution to the young president's enterprise opened into the world of athletic-star money management. Why would a hedge fund-of-funds mysterious as any criminal cartel specialize in juiced jocks? What, if any, was the criminal element behind the mysteriously bland-seeming group of Managing Partners in the Caymans? Why did accountants to the stars steer them to this fund, whose performance trailed that of many popular mutual funds? Were Seamus to answer these questions he might resolve many mysteries.

Good old Bob and his wife live the good life to perfection. From their autos to their clothing to their appliances to the automated devices that facilitate the family's learning and entertainment, their life-style is a perfection they continuously upgrade. Most Sundays Mom, Dad and the boys enjoy Sunday dinner at the Little Italian after Mass.

The Jackhammer continues to rule the Mafia and to manipulate the politics of New Jersey undisturbed. No one knows how much he knows about this case: he is a swamp into which human affairs sink.

Does he care that one of three persons on earth who could bring him and his crew down shares his bed, legs bent back by her muscular personal trainer, beside her vials of prescriptions? Another loyally fights the law. The last chants in Tibet, concentrating on the spirit entering and leaving his body through nostrils dry from the altitude.

Mikie Mont was sick of the world's curiosity about his medical supplements and his sexual preference. Early as the fifth grade he knew his talent at and behind the plate would be his tickets away from his family. He knew from Pop Warner League, when his father would show up in a limo accompanied by lithe heavy men in leather jackets, that his Dad was different from other dads. He saw the pitchers setting him up with fat ones down the middle. He winced when fielders booted his grounders, and his coaches went crazy telling his Dad about Mikie's exploits. For he sensed that he would have no friends if this kept up: it was tough enough being the best player by far, now he had to suffer from the world's fear of his father.

His mother was no help. On the few occasions when his father stayed at their gated mansion in Orange, she needled the big man or screamed at him so continuously that meals were unbearable, and Mikie would plead and plead to be excused until finally he'd leave unnoticed. In the sixth grade he came home to find her doing what he and other boys called the hula-hula with a small bald man swathed in black hair. He believed her when she told him she would have him killed if he ever told anyone about it. The next day she gave him a dog, a Doberman pincher that showed Mikie no affection, was unresponsive when Mikie tried to teach him games, and was run over chasing one of Mikie's few visitors from the front gate. Mikie ran after the dog, and the car that wiped the dog out grazed Mikie's left arm. A week later Mikie's Mom screamed at him, "How am I supposed to have any friends if the neighbors get killed for running over that dog you never took care of and you running into the street into traffic?"

His father set him up in the back yard with a batting cage and a pitching machine, and in the basement with a state-of-the-art Cybex circuit, a complete home entertainment system, and tapes of World Series and Yankees highlights from the last 5 decades. When it was clear Mikie's piston legs, his uncanny tolerance of pain, his sense of baseball strategy, his rifle-throws to second were leading him to be a star catcher, his father arranged for weekly private coaching sessions in the back yard with Yogi Berra, who told him, "You can be even greater than I was if you take care of your legs and keep your hands off the bimbos."

Mikie's younger sister went to Catholic schools because they taught girls how to be good girls and because their inferior athletic programs didn't bother girls. She was quiet, skinny, and plain until age 15, when suddenly she bloomed into such a beauty that her parents sent her to Catholic boarding school where the nuns would protect her from boys. She broke every possible sports record at her school by Junior year, but her parents never visited her or showed interest in her exploits, and she refused to meet with college recruiters, settling for an admin assistant's job in a huge chemical company headquarters. She and Mikie lost track of each other, and then she was dead.

Mikie followed Yogi's advice to develop his career slowly —"You'll go faster if you take it slow"—and he went to Rutgers where he studied art history and brought that college's baseball program national renown, if not a championship. He grew tired of reporters asking him how it felt to "carry the team on his back." He filled his sketchbooks with nightmarish creatures that seemed like an addict's twisted dream of jungle plants and jungle rodents, but he never took a drink or got high as an undergraduate.

His father assigned Yogi to negotiate with the tens of franchises that wanted Mikie in their fast-track farm systems, but Mikie insisted on a far-West team, and settled for Rupert Murdock's niggling offer to join the Dodgers, where the rest is history, a history that passed in front of Mikie like a documentary of someone else's life until his rbi totals dropped below 90, his homers into the teens, and his batting average below 290. At this point George Steinbrenner sought to bring him to the Yankees, but after conferring with Yogi, who salted his advice with the first profanity he had unloaded on Mikie in his 15 years as mentor ("That asshole thinks he's a big dick, but he's just a little prick"), Mikie took a lowball offer from the Mets, amidst a storm of cacophonous punditry.

The jars of green pills behind the bandages in the Dodgers' dressing room never tempted Mikie, who slept regular hours, worked out off-season, and avoided, as his mentor suggested, even the tastiest bimbos that seemed to generate themselves like sprites and nymphs from the wide beachfront before his Malibu home. Mikie drove a simple Japanese sedan, appeared at a minimum of charitable functions, and politely refused all social contact with his father's associates in entertainment studios, racetracks, and Las Vegas. He had neither seen nor heard from his mother or father since the days of his brief visits home during college.

He was called the most eligible bachelor in California sports, but his name was never coupled with those of any women in the print or video tabloids.

In his whole life, he had had only one true friend, an intense, long-haired computer geek, who pulled the fast one on Mikie's college teammates and other jocks. The long-haired geek shared the anguish he suffered from his digital mentor's betrayal, shared the beginnings of his spiritual quest with Mikie, for whom these intense discussions at a New Brunswick teahouse were like replacement sparkplugs for the missing cylinders in the engine of his consciousness. They told stories of their difficult mothers, and the geek was the only person on earth to whom Mikie divulged his exasperation, anger and fear at being the son of a Mafia don whose surname he no longer used in full. Occasionally they flirted.

Mikie's life unconsciously illustrated Gilbert Sorrentino's encomium on the purity of baseball, a sport requiring a minimum of contact between opponents, a sport emphasizing the music of geometry and physics. For Mikie's devotion to baseball was the devotion of a novice, a monk, an abbot, and a saint.

It embittered him that the speculation about his sexuality eliminated his cherished goal: to redeem inner-city boys through baseball.

Bitterness at losing his dream of saving boys from the miseries he'd experienced, at the persistent rumors of his homosexuality, at his loveless existence, led him to play for the Mets with the fury of desperation. But as the crouching and the pounding took its toll upon his legs, feet, hips and hands, his numbers slipped even further than they had in Los Angeles, and his devotion to the workouts that had kept him ahead of his competitors waned. But he wanted above all else to show the world that was scorning him (every time he struck or grounded out, he heard, "Fag! Fag") he could still be MVP. And so he hired a personal trainer who knew his way around supplements, and was as handy with a needle as a weight station. Mikie knew this could be suicide, but he wanted it, he wanted out.

He wondered where steroids had been all his life. His workouts became more exhilarating than circling the bases or catching the leadoff batter stealing second. The sight of his bulging muscles, his amazing ass, the upward curve of his Vo2 max were ecstasy. But after the game, no matter how great a showcase for him, he found himself angry and snappy with the reporters. He raged at the Queens traffic. He wrote a check to a Ronkonkoma dealership for a black Hummer with tinted windows. It was relief to roar the engine at smaller cars while blasting rap music on his state-of-the art stereo, but when he got to his condo in Great Neck he was unable to stop the seething, could not sleep without drinking a pint of gin mixed with lowfat milk. He spent restless hours with gay and straight porn, but was unable to pleasure himself before falling into a stupor that seemed to last 5 minutes before the alarm rang. He drove to clubs in lower Manhattan, where his black military vehicle became a landmark, and once he went home with a young woman who'd rescued him from hurting two drunken fans who made jokes about which end of the bat he used and where, but all he could do was snivel and moan into her lap. The big car became dilapidated and required frequent repairs as Mikie fell asleep under viaducts on both sides of the East River, and as he scraped pillars and walls in his manic urge to get going despite the miasma of obstacles the great city seemed to place before him above all others.

Suddenly his MVP season took a nosedive. A *Daily News* pundit gave unforgiving fans new fuel when he pronounced Mikie's season "maniac depressive."

His batting average plunged below 280, and after an August goose-egg day at the plate, he stormed into the press room and throttled a reporter who'd written kind words about his community service donations.

"You can't call me a fag, you little prick."

It took 4 security guards to pull him from the prostrate veteran reporter, who'd praised Mikie's "good heart" and his "dignified sense of privacy that never left him, whether his numbers went up or down."

The League suspended Mikie for the balance of the season and required inpatient treatment for drug dependency. The reporter declined to sue.

-9-

If you want a game thrown, get to the pitcher and catcher. Sure, you can persuade batters to lie down, fielders to miss plays, but it's not easy to smell it when the catcher's calling a dumb game and the pitcher's putting it where the batters like it. I call it insurance when I have #1 and #2 in the bag. So when Mikie Mont starts using one of our trainers to get juiced, I'm watching. When he goes to the rehab our insurance company owns, I'm happy. Two weeks into his program I pay him a little visit upstate, but the big fag is too doped up or just too stupid to understand how we can beat the odds bigtime, and the night of my visit upstate I'm drinking in the club bar by the Canal off Third when I get a call the Boss wants to see me. I'm happy about that till I get to his office behind the repair shop in Bay Ridge and instead of "How's business, Joey," for which I have a good answer ready, he head-butts me over the eye, gives me a forearm to the throat, and the bleeding and the wheezing are killing me so bad I don't get what he's screaming until the "assholes" and "cocksuckers" slow down and I hear, "Don't you know who Mikie is, you piece of shit?" And when he tells me I'm almost begging him to beat me some more just so I stay alive because I don't want to die before I pay off my book debts and leave my old lady in the clear. Or I'm thinking Witness Protection. When you hit the wall the wall wins.

-10-

I can't stand Tibet. Why did I think it so cool to be a monk? I've been vegetarian for years, but that doesn't mean I lived on white rice seasoned by white rice. If the athletes and movie stars hadn't taken over this place, I might have gone back to the States for good food, running water, and clean clothes. I guess I'm a little like poor kids who believe the military recruiters and then hit basic training and get sent to Iraq and Iran. No matter what my danger, I would have gone back to normal living if Richard Gere, Phil Jackson and all of them hadn't led our Master to tone the place up. Now we have laptops and play stations, a hearty balanced vegan diet. I hate the press and film crews ordering us around—we call the preparations for a big name's advent "Gere-ing up, " and I tell myself that the limit will be when Barbra Streisand begins to lead the chants. But the celebs are a necessary evil if we are to maintain our new level of amenities.

Now I am free to wander the amazing landscape every day for hours, pondering my goals in life.

-11-

Mikie Mont wore the Arms Acres T shirts more happily than he'd worn any uniform. Once his withdrawal from the medley of stimulants, sedatives, and hormone enhancers that would have killed a weaker body was complete, he stopped crying and sulking and began to listen to the hopeful things his counselors and his fellow-addicts were saying. Two things were weird: he believed what people were telling him, and he felt that his semi-private cot and the ugly green corridors filled with people so ordinary he wanted to spit on them when he was high and to hug them when his head cleared and he was able to sleep unaided—that these unprepossessing physical and human circumstances were his first home on earth. He was proud to be in Group 6, and convinced the Group 6 nurse, an inarticulate black man who stumbled along with the jargon of the counselors, was the kindest heart in the Acres. The social worker, a short aggressive Jewish woman, who, whenever Mikie tried to describe a situation, called on members of the group to get up and help him "sculpt" it, was the strongest soul on earth. When she took his family history, her questions were the most profoundly far-reaching he'd heard, and the family tree she designed with him was artwork beyond any trees of Jesse he'd seen in church. He cried inwardly and often outwardly at the stories of spousal or parental neglect endured by his group-mates, he forgave them for the bad and dumb things they'd done to themselves or others, and he never wanted to leave his home group or the Acres.

Visitors from his team or from the world of business went by in a vague whirl. He expected no visits from his family, and there were none.

The nurse began to prod Mikie to attend the 12th-step meetings more regularly. He told Mikie that he was a graduate of The Acres, and that he'd been clean and sober for 12 years. And because he loved the nurse, Mikie joined Alcoholics Anonymous. The social worker gave him the greater New York AA meeting book, dropping Mikie's spirits by telling him he's leave the facility soon, but raising them by saying she could see him as a private patient, and that if he went to the meetings and stayed clean, he would regain his self-esteem.

Mikie ran from the session with the social worker to the nurse.

"Joe, Joe, I've got to leave soon. I don't want to leave. I'm scared to leave."

"Mikie, separation anxiety, man. That's normal, man."

"But I'm all alone, I don't know what to do."

"You've got the program, man. The program, it's like a surrogate mother and father. Shoot, my Mom's a junkie and I never had no Dad, man, but I've got my program and my self-esteem, man."

"I'm scared, Joe. You really think I'll be OK?"

"You've got to trust the man with the plan, that's God, Mike. You think He can't figure this out?"

When Mikie left the rehab he was 10 pounds heavier from all the cake and junk foods, and he had the beginnings of an addiction to coffee. His emotions raced from high to low like a roller-coaster, but he knew that his suspension gave him freedom to go to as many meetings as he needed.

He was almost relieved to learn of the collapse of the hedge fund to which he had entrusted the preponderance of his assets on the advice of his personal trainer who told him it could only go up. He had just enough to live on without his baseball salary.

12

Elliot Spitter wanted to stay alive. He could be of no use to the public if he hounded the Mafia the way he hounded Wall Street and the insurance industry, for he could be rubbed out and never run for governor. The young lawyers who spurred themselves and each other to follow leads and develop cases for the crusading attorney-general, subsisting as they put it on a diet of work, caffeine and triathalons, could not fathom their hero-chief's reluctance to cut off the mob tentacles grasping unions, finance, politics, and a few resigned to join white-shoe law firms in protest.

And so the eyes of his staff were trained on the wiry body and the firm jaw of the AG when the fund they knew stank to high heaven—The Beautiful People Fund of the Caymans—pulled its vanishing act, reducing household names in sports and entertainment to financial ruin. What would the Teddy Roosevelt, the Tom Dewey of our day do with the headlines echoing about his chiseled cranium?

The nurse and the social worker became Mikie's mother and father. It was a necessary transference, for Mikie never had a Dad to reassure him when he was unable to live up to his mother's guidance or a mother to provide the guidance. The nurse became his easy-going sponsor in Alcoholics Anonymous, and the social worker became his hard-driving counselor, impatient with his complaints about his family, insisting on rubbing his nose in his sexuality.

Dominant animals never take their eye off the ball. They take no time off to bask in contemplation or celebration of their superior strength, stamina, agility: dominance is achieved by relentless, repetitious acts of aggression and intimidation. A dominant animal never rests.

Enrico (The Jackhammer) Montevenero knew it would be lonely at the top, but he was ready. He'd watched too many mob leaders turn into pussies and get caught or shot. He was always ready to kill and maim to attain his objectives, but he knew he needed to find instruments of control or torture beyond violence, and when he sought out a fate worse than death his dominating instincts led him to the insight that made him king: *Their balls are in their wallets.*

The Jackhammer read *The Wall Street Journal* and *Money Magazine.* He knew that of the traditional sources of Mob revenue-- gambling, pornography, prostitution, extortion, embezzlement, and drug-dealing—only gambling and drug-dealing were truly growth industries. He was pissed at his motherfucker partners Trump and Griffin for screwing up so badly in Atlantic City; he knew enough about global warming to stay away from riverboat casinos; and he was content with the return on his 5% ownership of Las Vegas. The minority stake in Vegas put him in harmonious contact with his peers, and he liked to pick their brains occasionally, though he never let them know that was what he was doing.

And drugs: drugs were crazy. How could you find a reliable source in all those fucked-up South American and Mideast countries?

The jackhammer believed in vertical integration, and he hated a business dependent on loco cartels and dictators propped up by the idiot CIA. He needed his own dictator.

But where else could he grow?

The answer was blatant, ubiquitous: entertainment. Stars and players sitting on top of a global growth industry dominated by a nation addicted to distracting itself. He loved it. He began to bankroll, through investment banks that managed his unions' pension plans, movies and tv series on organized crime by Coppula and other prominent directors. He studied the balance sheets of independent and corporate-owned sports franchises. And he counted on his son's baseball career to afford his crew opportunities to network with sports figures.

-15-

That fucking fat dago yells at me about my pills. He's too stupid to know he drove me to them. We had a deal: I'd stay home and do the traditional Italian family thing, and he'd be faithful and be a real father and husband. I'd take care of my looks, not like those fat mamas that drive the goombas to bimbos, and I'd keep the house perfect.and he'd keep his pecker in his pants. Not that he was any goddam gift as a lover; I've known plenty better, Bob, my Bob above all. But I was OK with the deal until he started spending nights away and his goddam underwear started smelling like pussy. So two can play *that* game I thought. Yeah, that's what I thought until we had our "little sitdown." The cocksucker just outs and tells me he can do what he wants because of who he is but if I do he'll arrange an accident for me, maybe in the gym, maybe in my car. He tells me there's plenty of women who'll be better mothers to my babies. I tell the pencil dick he's welcome to any girl or boy he wants and he'd better kill me right now because if he doesn't my next call is the FBI. He screams I can't do that, and I start walking to the phone. He says, "Ok, how about this: you do whatever you want, I do whatever I want, but you be careful because I can take care of anyone or anything," and he shows me a picture of my personal trainer in his white gym suit in a pool of blood. The poor kid, he was gay, and the only thing he wanted to get into was my wardrobe.

-16-

In therapy Mikie learned that mistrust is self-pity that isolates you from yourself and prevents you from getting on with your life. He learned that love is hard work, but worth it. He received no guidance on whether to pursue men or women, "It makes no difference, humans are humans, and if you spend your time wondering what you want not going for it, you'll be the same old withdrawn Mikie that almost killed himself. I don't care what you do with your genitals, as long as you take precautions." That kind of talk hurt Mikie's feelings and made him want to quit therapy.

But after he'd been sober six months he found himself in a morning meeting staring at a long-haired man in shorts and a tanktop, and the long-haired man caught him staring and asked him out for coffee anyplace but Starbucks. Mikie had moved into Park Slope because there were so many meetings you could walk to, and the long-haired man led him to the coffee bar at the back of the Community Bookstore. A famous novelist Mikie knew from the meetings pulled up to the store on his skateboard. A soft-spoken intelligent young man he knew from the meetings was putting books away. A bearded man was denouncing the President to a woman whose wild hair mixed her natural gray with the red, blond, and orange dyes she'd tried over the years of its growth, horizontal stripes that reminded Mikie he had once loved archeology. For the second time in his life Mikie felt at home on earth, an overwhelming joyful sensation, and he realized as he looked at the long-haired man's legs and ass that he was in love.

-17-

Seamus Heaney thought that Elliott Spitter was an asshole. *The motherfucker negotiates with his targets fucking jogging in Central Park? These protestant pussies act tough, but they're just playing games and running for office, and if Spitter goes after the Beautiful People Fund, I'll eat my wallet. Fuck I'd like to eat Daley's wallet, but that guy's too smart to let his private deals get near his public career.*

Seamus realized he was jealous of Spitter's fame, and of the staff that enabled Spitter to get to the bottom of cases. Seamus knew he could crack the Money Master Murder case if he had resources, and he knew he'd fry some big fishes if he did. And the connection between his murder and Spitter's potential case against the Beautiful People's Fund tantalized Seamus like the vision of the Virgin Mary his grandmother in Cicero kept claiming when he brought his bored family to her yellow-siding house.

There must be thousands of ambitious policemen hoping to crack the cases that would bring down the pretty faces in the news, policemen whose genetic code slapped ugly ethnic mugs on their crania, but whose brains whizzed far more efficiently than those behind prettier faces adorning the crania at the top. They struggled through life without access to the lithe slender bodies in places like the East Bank Club, the dowdy clothing and the fat arms of their mates an eternal social judgment. Only two men in history have combined ugly mugs with social refinement: Humphrey Bogart and Jean Paul Belmondo, and they were Seamus' heroes, to the puzzlement of his family, friends, and colleagues.

-18-

Mikie's sponsor and his therapist told him he should avoid serious relationships until he was sober at least a year. Dating was fine, but no commitments or sex. That was a relief to Mikie, who knew that the passion kindled in the bookstore could prove a challenge greater than drugs and baseball. The big difference was he wanted this challenge more than anything, with his whole natural being.

-19-

When the Jackhammer wished he could find his own dictator, he had little hope his wish would come true. But one day his investment banker from CitiCorp told him that Chile was an economic miracle wrought by the god of modern economics, Milton Friedman. The investment banker, hyper-aggressive because he toiled at a large bank rather than a true investment bank and because he attended Rutgers rather than one of the Big Three Ivies, was the only banker Enrico worked with gutsy enough to use the word "Mafia." Enrico gave him business because he sensed that the tonier bankers despised him as they rang up the big fees he generated. He despised them too, but he needed as many ladies and gentlemen in his professional life as Wall Street could afford him.

The Rutgers boy introduced Enrico to hedge funds, and soon the Jackhammer's ROI jumped from 11% to 17%. And he found Enrico his dictator.

It is difficult for a deposed dictator to preserve the wealth he has extracted from his country. He may maintain ties with the generals and colonels who put him into office, who created the steady flow of corpses that kept him in power. He may have been convicted of no crimes, and the business community of his native shores may long for the order and logic of his rule. But the international banking system's computers are like the conscience free market-practices must ignore to remain free, and wealthy dictators run easily but hide their billions less easily, particularly dictators whose drive and ambition make it difficult for them to restrict their restless economic strivings to Monaco or Caribbean Islands.

And since Augusto Pinochet continued a major presence on the world stage, feted especially by Great Britain's metallic female Winston Churchill, he was galled by his inability to evade the global funds transfer systems, and to grow his wealth in peace. It frustrated him mightily that his generals and colonels controlled the coca cash crop, but that he could not benefit from the generous land-grants with which he had secured their loyalty. He entertained a series of proposals from investment bankers who thronged his sumptuous quarters in Spain and Great Britain, but no one could solve the problem at which he could only hint until an unmannerly young man from CitiCorp introduced him to an underground economy whose power unleashed the dictator's measly rate of return. In his gratitude he gave the young Rutgers graduate his signed first edition of *Money is Freedom,* by the Nobel Laureate from Chicago.

But the unmannerly banker was asked to leave the room when the Jackhammer and his dictator had their first sitdown at a location he was assured he would lose his genitals or his life for divulging.

-20-

When I was 12 and beginning to get looks from the boys in the school across the street I decided they were a lot more exciting than a bunch of girls giggling in braces, and I began to let the best-looking guys dry hump me. Jesus how they screamed and cried when they came. I lay there with my legs spread thinking there's something in this dirty stuff, something strong that turns boys into girls. Then I got tired of them having all the fun and I taught them how to finger me. I was too smart to give it away until freshman year in college when I stole my roommate's guy by fucking him while she held out. The sex was fun, but it was more fun to watch her crack up and leave school.

I never saw why it was such a big deal whether a guy stuck his piece of meat into my hole. Sometimes it was fun, other times boring, but it was never a big deal. Then I met Enrico. I knew who he was from the papers, and I thought well maybe this one won't be boring. He wasn't: he'd already killed five guys, he told me. He told me he was already worth ten million. He told me these things because he loved me, and he wanted to see how I'd feel. I felt good. But when most men would put the move on, he told me he wanted to marry a virgin, and asked me if I was pure, and you know what I said. He told me that when we married he'd have to kill me if I ever told anyone anything I knew. That felt good too: finally something was exciting in my life.

So we get married and we get the big house and he becomes the big boss and I've got to say it was all pretty boring and the most boring part was in bed, but that was no big deal until I met Bobbie eating lunch alone at the Little Italian, and there was something about his deep voice and his shiny head and all that dark hair on his face that made me want to ball him right there on the red tablecloth. And when he got his shirt off in room 20 at the Qualiity Inn on Route 17 and I saw all that hair I melted like I'd never dreamed of melting. The sheets were dripping and the room smelt like a gym. It was like I was breathing sex.

-21-

I've used no intoxicants since my college weekends with the mentor who betrayed me. The pleasures of the mind far exceeded the rush and the giggles the noble weed gave me, and when to the pleasures of the mind I added the more pure and exquisite pleasures of meditation and contemplation of universal wholeness, I had, until I arrived here in Tibet, all the pleasure I thought I would ever need. And so I arrived at this spiritual source expecting a refined joy I would breathe until my spirit migrated from my body, but I have found that humiliation and ritual do not cause higher pleasures to absorb my being. Tibet was a bummer until I could walk and dream alone, and what has entered my being so profoundly I want to cry out to the far cliffs is the realization I have ignored love, that amazing being that stares most humans in the face until they flinch from its strong regard, and dissipate it into lust, jealousy, anger. But I am at last ready for love, I know, and as I wander these ancient trails I realize its mystical but sensual ecstasy is my destiny. I realize.

As I descended towards the village, a tall strong man from my past strode up the trail with a smile so bright I cried.

-22-

Perhaps—since they told me only the highlights, we'll never really know-- the most exquisite pleasure of Mikie and Joseph's lovemaking was their giggling, snorting, and roaring with laughter while physically entangled. The Best Western's Quiet Comfort Series had appeared in their once-modest village, a perfect honeymoon-spot for men of straightened means. In scores of raptly exploratory positions they found themselves unable to cease giggling over little lines featuring "Worst Western" and "Best Eastern." A man there to service their mini-bar happened upon them and withdrew in a quiet consternation they compared to Cortes, "silent upon a prick in Darien," and to twenty variants of Moses and the burning bush-- flaming pansies, burning faggots, humping hollyhocks, gloves off the fox, up in smoke, we are what we are, no you are, yes I am, maybe you're not, fucking around the campfire, boy sprouts, sizzling wieners, mellow marshes, hairy prophets, Charlton Hairstyle, the parting of the red face, burning tushies, here's smoke in your eyes, hot buttered come, smoked Buddhist bologna, and say that I Am sent you away happy.

For two men whose roots would always be New Jersey, it was a modern wonder they had needed to find Tibet to get laid.

-23-

Elliot Spitter had studied female erogenous zones, and quizzed his wife on hers, so that he could always leave the bed satisfied he'd done a thorough job. Enrico Montevenero didn't give a flying fuck how the babes felt as long as they acted like they loved it. His assistants always instructed new babes carefully. The reliable chemics in the bodies of Good Old Bob and the former accountant fizzled when the boys arrived, but they both decided that screwing around was dangerous to their elaborate lifestyle. Despite her fat Irish arms and sloppy thighs, Seamus Heaney's old lady remained a great roll in the hay.

-24-

On the fourteenth day of their honeymoon, Mikie and Joseph decided to change the world. It was time to discuss something besides their next fuck, next walk, or next meal. The 12-step meetings in their village were suffused with a New Age mentality Mikie struggled to respect. And so they decided to return to the good old US of A, Mikie shaving his head, affecting flowing Eastern garb, and resuming his natal name. Joseph cut his hair, exchanged his contacts for glasses, dressed a neat business casual, and bought a powerful laptop. They found a garden apartment in Brooklyn.

They decided that the past cannot be undone, the fate to which our families subject us cannot be reversed, but that truth, justice, forgiveness, humor could go a long way towards affording mistreated mortals the serenity they now enjoyed—and that cutting the Jackhammer down to size could be great fun. They would "pool their resourcefuls" and see if they couldn't work some magic on the state lying across the dirty, cluttered harbor from their new home.

-25-

It is not impossible for two bodies in love making love to tell lies, inwards or outwards, but it is less likely than in other circumstances. The blindness of love could without paradox be called visionary, the blindness of justice a lie. I love both Joseph and Mikie, and I have a grudging affection for Seamus Heaney. I've not met the wife. As I take these three men forward, I fear for their lives. I fear for all our lives. Joseph and Mikie will venture where fools and derelicts tread. It's as if they received travel brochures for Caribbean islands and Rhine Cruises, but chose to wade barefoot in the suppurating waters of the Meadowlands for holiday sport—and you gentle reader are in a Jersey Central train looking down on the two idiots as you cuff your evening paper into shapes that will not intrude upon the stranger sharing your seat. It would never occur to *you* to erase the fate to which your genes, your family history, your work, the very limitations of your body have dictated. Why should it? And if you knew what good intentions fueled by love will lead Joseph and Mikie to, your contempt for their naiveté would heat to anger. And if you knew the stranger sharing your seat worked for Enrico Montevenero, you would allow your legs and your buttocks to go to sleep as you risked cramping your whole body by plastering it to the grey streaked window and its soiled frame.

-27-

"Why would you question that I, with my unbroken record of defending the consumers and investors of New York would pursue the perpetrators of the Beautiful People's Fund until I brought them to light and to earth? I have been amused by the news stories speculating I would hold back. Elliot Spitter never holds back. And when I am elected governor, my first phone call will be to my replacement AG to encourage him or her to get to the bottom of this sordid affair."

When the returns handed Spitter a victory more resounding than any poll or any pundit forecast, his first call was to his Hong Kong tailor, his second to his largest donor, his third to his prep school football coach, and his fourth to a high-end interior decorator willing to take on an old dump in Albany. For Spitter had promised to roll up his sleeves and make the governor's mansion his predecessors had shunned home, saving money for the taxpayers. His children had overcome the 907-to-1 odds against admission to the finest prep schools in Manhattan, and would remain in the hands of loveable alien caretakers from whose Spartan wages federal and state taxes plus FICA would be deducted while their parents turned the state around.

28

When the returns handed Spitter a victory more resounding than any poll or pundit forecast, The Jackhammer did not bother to call the young CitiCorp investment banker who'd stepped ahead of his colleagues on Wall Street to become Spitter's largest donor and most active fundraiser. He knew the young banker's pda prompted him to call his most powerful client weekly.

Below its throbbing surface, a modern city resembles a jumbled pile of bodies buried alive, a hecatomb ever-growing like a landfill on Staten Island. The impacted limbs, the crushed skeletal structures form the network connecting earthbound buildings, abandoned tunnels, intersected by gigantic stakes the superstructure in which we live drives into the earth and bedrock to steady itself. The still-beating hearts are the transformers implanted without thought to their useful remaining futures. And the veins and arteries so complex not even their makers can map them are the ever-more-sophisticated wiring and piping we need to energize the technology energizing our work and play.

Ever since he touched Mikie, Joseph had dreamed in words. Happily, he analyzed this strange and sometimes boring change from unconscious movie to unconscious caption as the healing of his soul by the beloved sight vouchsafed his sore Tibetan eyes.

He wondered whether to disclose these nocturnal dictations to his spouse, but he knew the dear boy would look for a cure—and might not these messages be from the very Ground of our Being he has sought from the beginning of his spiritual journey, and might not his feeling bored and pestered by them be the resistance so many prophets from Jonah to C.S. Lewis have felt to their being called?

For he knew that if he and his partner against crime were to succeed, it could be his intuitive explorations of wires and microprocessors that would lead them to the shrine of justice.

-30-

Mikie's dream began in *Camden, where scarfaced pugs were battling, as their managers put it, according to Marcus of Queensbaby, refraining from kidney and groin shots, leading with their sinister gloves not their shoulders and elbows, and when they got home after a day of following their perilous dreams without emolument, they listened to the angry railings of their scrimping spouses patiently, politely, and a chorus of sweet words from ugly faces promised to find compromises between breadwinning and their bloody ambitions.*

And every coal-fired plant was so effectively scrubbed and dampened that its emissions were no more toxic than the pantings of a large dog.

Along the Delaware River the aging colony of hippies in Flatbrookville turned to a natural high, and walked through the woods they had plucked of non-native plants hand-in-hand with children and grandchildren about whose real parentage they ceased to wonder or rankle, they were all so beautiful.

The mayor of Hoboken recently photographed asleep naked on his porch surrounded by a Stonehenge-like array of beer bottles and cans called his sponsor, returned to his home twelfth-step group, and joined the nearest Gold's gym, while without bitterness his wife and children did six months worth of his laundry and erased his voice messages from bars and whorehouses.

Squadcars on the Parkway, the Turnpike, and routes 17, 78, 80 and 287 pulled over upscale white speeders, searching their smooth upholsteries and hi-end sound systems for illegal substances and, refusing even the most romantic cash bribes, remanded them to slammers normally reserved for the racially-profiled.

Three extinct species of waterfowl were discovered in Seacaucus.

Nuns already hopelessly lost driving from their Brooklyn convent on a mission of mercy to the trailer people of Louisiana and Mississippi airports found a gas station looming seemingly from nothing in the Meadowlands. The owner threw down his pornographic reading to set them straight, and as they were thanking and blessing him, St. Francis rose from the fresh spring that bubbled through and around the owner's curse-laden asphalt patches and plugs, and the saint's rise through the pavement was hailed by a chorus of once-extinct tree-frogs whose ethereal rendition of the "Sanctus" from Palestrina's "Missa Papa Marceli" did indeed sanctify this New Age's rediscovery of plainsong.

Beaming clerks at tollstations handed out free passes to Jersey Transit and Erie-Lackawana trains.

Something told the Coney Island Polar Bear Club to do their thing in the Meadowlands, and the perfumed waters over which wafted a clean sea breeze from Staten Island that carried a thousand emanations from garage bands better even than the Badfinger or Etta James confirmed their pilgrimage seeking new waters to shock their brazen skins.

Urgent orders from every restaurant listed in Zagat's Guide to New York City, as well as in its miniscule New Jersey footnote, arrived at *dying family chicken farms.*

No bribes were offered to or solicited by public servants.

Cars idling on Route 80 West were abandoned for roadside Scrabble, Bocci, and Charades. Ski resorts in the Poconos groomed their artificial snow and stocked their lodge bars in vain, while yuppies who had never noticed places like Paterson enough to wonder what they were used their considerable aerobic fitness to explore urban landscapes and to chat with their natives.

No pesticides or chemical fertilizers were purchased anywhere in the Garden State.

Gun redemption sites became arsenals that could have menaced the independence of most U.S. client-states, and spilled over into precinct parking lots that came to resemble Western gun fairs.

There were 1221 football games scheduled that night, during which not one parent got drunk and threatened his team's coach, not one coach or trainer blew up at an erring player, the cheerleaders opted for modern dance routines designed by Cunningham and Tharp, the local vocal talent substituted "We Shall Overcome" for the "Star-Spangled Banner," the halftime bands played Ellington's sacred music, and everywhere could be heard parents comforting restless children and coaches comforting weeping athletes in a magically convincing susurrus of, it's not whether you win, it's how you play the game.

Her legs were freezing in the miniskirt but the dumb blond at Drew University knew that the only way to pass Anthro and become the first member of her family to earn a college degree was to meet the Professor that night in his office. She ran into him playing catch with his preteen son near the steps of Kean Hall, and he gave her the name of a graduate student who could tutor her for a nominal fee.

The food on the Amtrak trains climbing and descending New Jersey was superb.

The air smelled of the earth and its cooling and falling vegetation, and of the many rivers and wetlands that adorn the state.

It was a big night for sports at the Meadowlands arena, football outdoors and basketball indoors, and the Jets and Nets both lost, but you'd never know it from fans who ordered only sushi, salad, unbuttered popcorn and bottled water, or from players who found themselves enjoying games unmarred by fouls and trash talk, perhaps because coaches, trainers, and players had forgotten somehow to receive injections or ingest their pills. And there was no rush for the parking lot when hope ran out for the home heroes.

The Jewish teacher in the poorest part of Newark had hated his job, which consisted of subduing a group of 7th-grade boys and girls for whom contempt would be a mild word for the attitudes he expresses at his AFT meetings just in time for the period to end, but today he loved the children, who asked him to tell them about Paul Robeson and the idealism that had led him to choose teaching over computer science flooded him like the floods of being in Emerson's eyeball.

No lead or steel pellet whacked out a turkey in the country clubs of northern Bergen County. All the oversubscribed controlled hunts for which one could qualify only with a low-gage two-barrel gun worth more than $5000 purchased through the club's exclusive agency were canceled and the subscription money donated to CARE.

The feral cats and the monster rats in battling for turf at the Homeland Security Depot along the Raritan River curled up together for warmth as the night advanced.

(continues)

OTHER TITLES FROM AHADADA

Ahadada Books publishes poetry. Preserving the best of the small press tradition, we produce finely designed and crafted books.

Oulipoems (Philip Terry)   978-0-978-1414-2-4

Philip Terry was born in Belfast in 1962 and has been working with Oulipian and related writing practices for over twenty years. His lipogrammatic novel *The Book of Bachelors* (1999), was highly praised by the Oulipo: "Enormous rigour, great virtuosity—but that's the least of it." Currently he is Director of Creative Writing at the University of Essex, where he teaches a graduate course on the poetics of constraint. His work has been published in *Panurge*, *PN Review*, *Oasis*, *North American Review* and *Onedit*, and his books include the celebrated anthology of short stories *Ovid Metamorphosed* (2000) and *Fables of Aesop* (2006). His translation of Raymond Queneau's last book of poems, *Elementary Morality*, is forthcoming from Carcanet. *Oulipoems* is his first book of poetry.

The Impossibility of Dreams (David Axelrod)   978-0-9781414-3-1

Writes Louis Simpson: "Whether Axelrod is reliving a moment of pleasure, or a time of bitterness and pain, the truth of his poetry is like life itself compelling." Dr. David B. Axelrod has published hundreds of articles and poems as well as sixteen books of poetry. Among his many grants and awards, he is recipient of three Fulbright Awards including his being the first official Fulbright Poet-in-Residence in the People's Republic of China . He was featured in *Newsday* as a "Star in his academic galaxy," and characterized by the *New York Times* as "A Treat." His poetry has been translated into fourteen languages and he is a frequent and celebrated master teacher.

Now Showing (Jim Daniels)   0-9781414-1-5

Of Jim Daniels, the *Harvard Review* writes, "Although Daniels' verse is thematically dark, the energy and beauty of his language and his often brilliant use of irony affirm that a lighter side exists. This poet has already found his voice. And he speaks with that rare urgency that demands we listen." This is affirmed by Carol Muske, who identifies the "melancholy sweetness" running through these poems that identifies him as "a poet born to praise".

China Notes & The Treasures of Dunhuang (Jerome Rothenberg)   0-9732233-9-1

"*The China Notes* come from a trip in 2002 that brought us out as far as the Gobi Desert & allowed me to see some of the changes & continuities throughout the country. I was traveling with poet & scholar Wai-lim Yip & had a chance to read poetry in five or six cities & to observe things as part of an ongoing discourse with Wai-lim & others. The ancient beauty of some of what we saw played out against the theme park quality of other simulacra of the past....A sense of beckoning wilderness/wildness in a landscape already cut into to serve the human need for power & control." So Jerome Rothenberg describes the events behind the poems in this small volume—a continuation of his lifelong exploration of poetry and the search for a language to invoke the newness and strangeness both of what we observe and what we can imagine.

The Passion of Phineas Gage & Selected Poems (Jesse Glass)   0-9732233-8-3

The Passion of Phineas Gage & Selected Poems presents the best of Glass' experimental writing in a single volume. Glass' ground-breaking work has been hailed by poets as diverse as Jerome Rothenberg, William Bronk and Jim Daniels for its insight into human nature and its exploration of forms. Glass uses the tools of postmodernism: collaging, fragmentation, and Oulipo-like processes along with a keen understanding of poetic forms and traditions that stretches back to Beowulf and beyond. Moreover, Glass finds his subject matter in larger-than-life figures like Phineas Gage—the man whose life was changed in an instant when an iron bar was sent rocketing through his brain in a freak accident—as well as in ants processing up a wall in time to harpsichord music in order to steal salt crystals from the inner lip of a cowrie shell. The range and ambition of his work sets it apart. The product of over 30 years of engagement with the avant-garde, *The Passion of Phineas Gage & Selected Poems* is the work of a mature poet who continues to reinvent himself with every text he produces.

www.ahadadabooks.com

Secret, but Kept it Room (Mike Gubser)   0-9732233-7-5

Secret, but Kept it Room explores the development and stasis over time of self as image—at once real and artificial, subjective and perspectival, engaged in the physical world and torn from it, a self often disappearing into non-self. Mike Gubser treats the art of poetry as, in some sense, the art of experiment and problem-solving by placing the notion of self in various contexts—romance, depression, friendship, travel, memory, isolation—and poetic forms—visual, musical, lyrical modernist, numeric—to see how it reacts.

At That (Skip Fox)   0-9732233-6-7

Skip Fox, with the concern of an entomologist, presents passages sprawling and pinned in a shadow box of observations and odd lots. Framed under double glass, the mounting board of *At That* writhes with a cast of freaks: Ezekiel in the streets, a kitty bomb squad, sadists on steroids, the shadow of Cadmus, kingfishers, omen clad apertures of evening with cicada wings, heart attacks of clouds rolling in off the Gulf, a city mouse, spastic proctologists, and so forth, all projecting their "goods" in spate: smatterings, obsolete creeds, mordacious stumps, "furious opinions, exaggerations, fabrications," neo-prophetic stylings, verbal molestations, elegiac mumblings, the silence above a shallow grave, etc.

Ahadada Reader I (Alan Halsey, John Byrum, Geraldine Monk)   0-9732233-3-2

Combines the lively, challenging work of three experimental poets: Alan Halsey, John Byrum, and Geraldine Monk. Halsey's group of poems resurrects past versions of English, turning with peculiar spellings and striking frictions of their grammar. Byrum's work, entitled 'Approximations,' is a shifting visual text work mainly utilizing the text block, pointing to the form of a word as art itself. The final selection of Monk's work rounds out the book with her varying forms and sharply constructed lines.

the time at the end of this writing (Paolo Javier)   0-9732233-2-4

In his first poetry collection, Paolo Javier overlaps life in New York with his childhood spent in Manila and Cairo and imagined senior years referred to as "The Lid To The Great Jar." Javier's poems sail over the handlebars of a Huffy bicycle; saunter through the city onto balconies with lovers; respond to the visual art of Manuel Ocampo; and curse a botched reading of Tagalog. Of this book, Anselm Berrigan writes, "Perceptive poems; that there is pleasure despite never knowing what might happen next is no small part of what they know."

Investigations (Márton Koppány)   0-9732233-1-6

Marton Koppany is a poet, translator, and editor living in Budapest, Hungary. During the last few years he has been working on different collections of "experimental" poetry. The pieces comprising *Investigations* were written and published in the 80s and 90s, and exhibited/performed at Woodland Pattern Book Center, Milwaukee. Writes Karl Young : "Koppany's acute sense of the problems of language has moved him to try to get as close to the patterns of thought and perception as possible, and to create work that can be read by people who don't speak the language in which he writes, be it Hungarian or English"

Strange Currencies (Daniel Sendecki)   0-9732233-0-8

Writes Susan Ioannou: "In *Strange Currencies*, Daniel Sendecki travels through a Far East of haunting contrasts, where 'Roadside children collect lotus flowers to weave into bracelets' while feet away are landmines 'like knives asleep in kitchen drawers imagining meat.' Startling perceptions of past and present, teeming streets and loneliness, killing fields and open sky are juxtaposed in finely textured images, drawing us to touch the mystery hidden between 'the agony and beauty.' How refreshing to read poems that 'Make myself as small as possible' and reach outward, not only to look closely at a far corner of the world, but through it, for glimpses of enduring value—'to see a little light.'

www.ahadadabooks.com

ahadada

books

Send a request to be added to our mailing list:
http://www.ahadadabooks.com/

Ahadada Books are available from these fine distributors:

Canada
Ahadada Books
3158 Bentworth Drive
Burlington, Ontario
Canada, L7M 1M2
Phone: (905) 617-7754
http://www.ahadadabooks.com

United States of America
Small Press Distribution
1341 Seventh Street
Berkeley, CA 94710-1409
Phone: (510) 524-1668
Fax: (510) 524-0852
http://www.spdbooks.org/

Europe
West House Books
40 Crescent Road
Nether Edge, Sheffield
United Kingdom S7 1HN
Phone: 0114-2586035
http://www.westhousebooks.co.uk/

Japan
Intercontinental Marketing Corp.
Centre Building 2nd floor
1-14-13 Iriya, Taitoku
Tokyo 110-0013
Telephone 81-3-3876-3073
http://www.imcbook.net/